I0596538

Other books by the author,

Catherine Wilcoxson

The Adventures of Captain Heman Kenney and Lady Catherine 1833-1917

Open Doors and Open Windows: A Journey with God

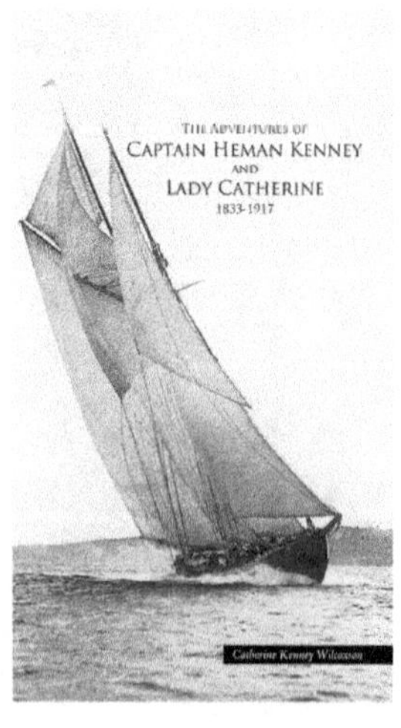

Don't Forget Maude:
The Tale of Two Sisters

Catherine Wilcoxson

Watt Light Publishing Company
404 LeBlanc Street
DeQuincy, LA 70633
Author's Email: cawilcoxson@theladycatherinecompany.com
Website: www.theladycatherinecompany.com

Graphic Design by Paul and Catherine Wilcoxson
Book Cover Design by Paul and Catherine Wilcoxson
Editor: Christopher Wilcoxson

Library of Congress Control Number: 2017907201

Publisher's Cataloging-in-Publication data
Wilcoxson, Catherine 1952-
Don't Forget Maude: The Tale of Two Sisters
Sequel to *The Adventures of Captain Heman Kenney and Lady Catherine – 1833-1917*
First Edition: June 2017
DeQuincy, Louisiana
Watt Light Publishing Company
346 p.
Includes pictures and illustrations
978-0-9966807-1-4 – Paperback
978-0-9966807-2-1 -- Ebook

Subjects: 1. Historical reconstruction – actual persons and events –partially fiction – Archives, Nova Scotia, Canada 2. Mystery – family secrets 3. Sisters – family breakup 4. Murder – Sheet Harbour, Nova Scotia - shooting/axe 5. Trial – grand jury
6. Execution – hanging
Summary: The kindness of a father. The darkness in a young man's soul. One sister's unshakeable love and another's unforgiving heart. Each one's faith in themselves and in each other will be tested when the unthinkable and unexpected wave crashes into an already unstable home . . . when murder comes knocking at the door.

DEDICATION

As a young girl, I spent many memorable hours listening to stories at my grandmother's feet. How could I have known then that some of those stories were not true? While many, including myself, did not listen, Frannie Kenney knew the truth and was not afraid to expose the stories for the lies they were. This book and the truths within are dedicated to the memory of Frannie and her desire to repair the rift in the family tree, torn apart by two sisters long ago.

ACKNOWLEDGMENTS

To Paul, my wonderful husband, whom I lean on daily. He is there to hold me steady. Our broken hearts have melted together as one, stronger than ever before. The strong heart that we now have is only because of our relationship with our Lord Jesus Christ.

Christopher Paul Edward Wilcoxson, my editor, with him and his father's help, they have kept me on the right track and have made my book better in every way. Thank you.

Thank you to my friends who continually asked me, "Have you finished the book yet?" For without their encouragement, this book may not be finished. Life brings unexpected trials and, without God, it's easy to give up. I pray you may learn from the mistakes of the past.

Contents

Table of Figures

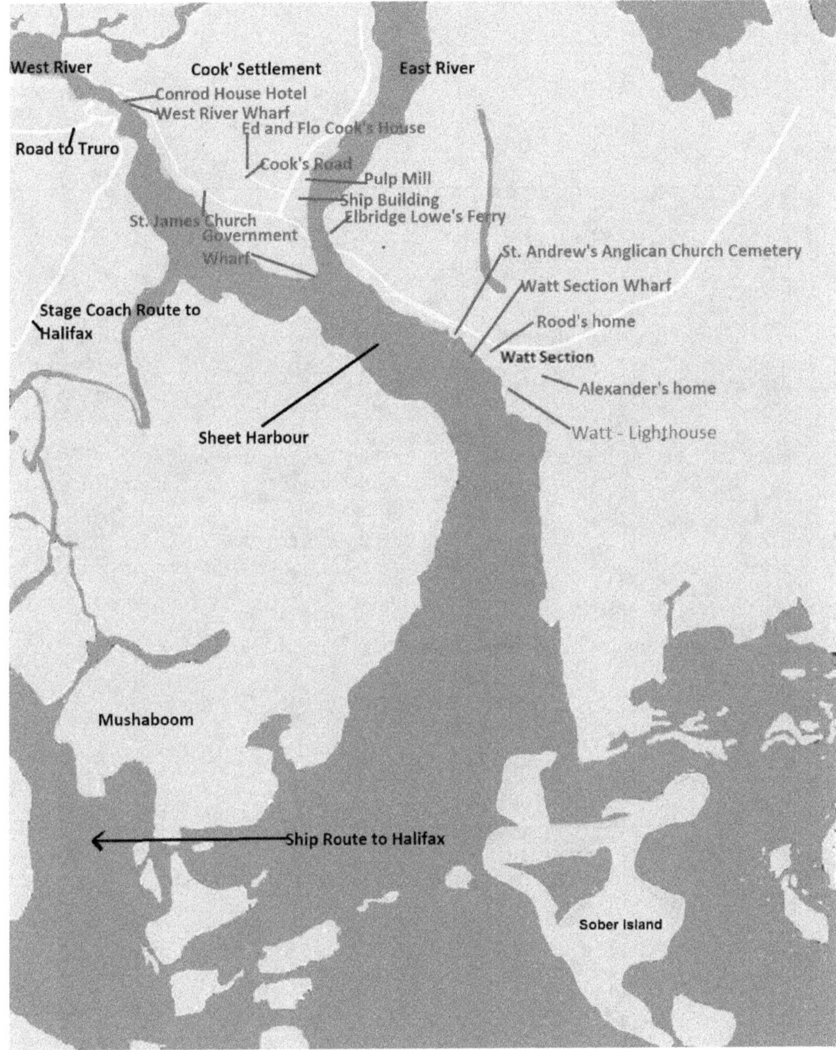

Figure 1: Map of Sheet Harbour

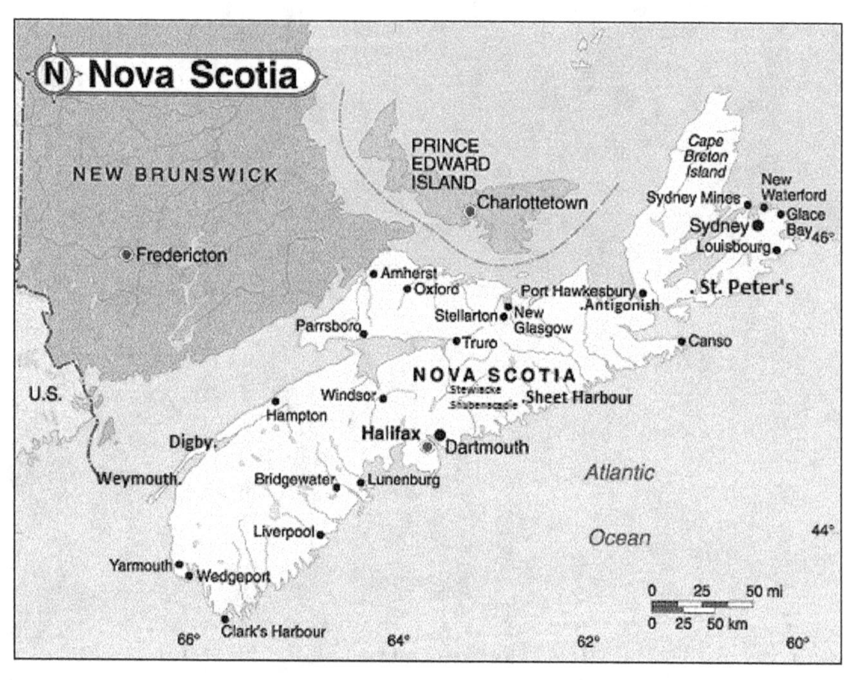

Figure 2: Map of Nova Scotia, Canada

Chapter One

Maude Was Calling

Catherine, come here. You've got to see this!"

Reaching for a gold tea towel, I wiped the water from my hands. "Now, dear? I'm cleaning potatoes for dinner."

I was already on my way across the kitchen, the tea towel still in my hand. Stepping down the two steps, which separated the kitchen from the TV room, I made my way to where Paul was sitting, staring at his computer screen.

He looked right up at me and pointed his index finger at the screen. "I found your grandmother's sister."

Paul's favorite pastime was genealogy. He has spent many hours trying to prove that David Crockett was a part of the Wilcoxson clan. A Captain John Cox's son, James Cox, a distant uncle of Paul, married Elizabeth Robertson, who is the daughter of Elizabeth Crockett, a distant cousin of David Crockett.

Paul's grandmother, Erma Powers Wilcoxson, who lived in Lawrenceburg, Tennessee, the same place where David Crockett lived, always told her grandsons that they were related to David Crockett. She had his rifle, unfortunately not Ole Betsy, his hunting horn, and bullet molds. Her grandsons were very impressed to be able to hold these items.

Genealogy is a slow-going project, Paul, growing tired of searching in the Wilcoxson clan, switched gears and started looking for the roots of the Kenney family tree.

Coming up to him sitting at his computer and focusing my eyes on the screen, I saw many people listed.

"Right there," Paul stabbed his finger on the computer screen, leaving a fingerprint.

My eyes finally focused on the name – Maude Cook Kenney.

All of a sudden, I sucked in air with a gasp.

"What is wrong, Catherine?" Paul knew that sound. If something startles me, I never scream. I just suck in air with a gasp.

"It can't be – Maude you say? I think I need to sit down." Turning around and groping for the over-stuffed brown loveseat, I fell into it with a clunk.

Everything seemed to move in slow motion. The walls, covered with my treasures from Nova Scotia, started to spin, slowly at first. I could see the pictures of Peggy's Cove Lighthouse begin to move. And the oar from the rowboat my father gave me, the fishnet, the buoys just above the lobster trap, followed suit. A hanging board painted blue, with a picture of a sailboat, which read 'welcome aboard' moved to the next wall, taking with it a plate inscribed with the map of Nova Scotia.

Everything was moving faster now. I placed my hands on my face, trying to stop the spinning, but it was no use. I was being taken somewhere in the back of my mind. But, where?

Maude. I knew that name. I had heard that name. Falling back in time, things slowed down. My mind was searching. Maude?

Yes, I remember. I was only seven or eight years old, but I remember. I was a tiny little thing with wheat-colored blond hair. Bangs framed my very large blue eyes that filled my little round face. I was sitting in a rocking chair, for there was more than one in the small room of the cottage, where my grandmother lived.

Sitting beside me was Grammy Kenney, rocking as she told me stories. I loved to hear her stories. Every morning during the summer, you would find me sitting beside her, listening to every word she spoke. Stories of sailing schooners, lighthouses, and even Indian attacks. Stories of when she was young and when she married Alexander, the son of Heman, the great schooner captain of the *Lady Catherine*.

We were sitting together in her small living room. She had pictures of her children and grandchildren on the wall. Sitting on a table beside her was a picture of her husband Alexander. It always amazed me how much it looked like my dad. She would laugh when I said that, for I said it often. The table in front of the window held her favourite fern. Her friends always told her she could grow the nicest ferns in Sheet Harbour. I believed it, since I believed everything that my Grammy told me.

We were talking about her lighthouse. "You had a lighthouse?" I asked.

"Yes, of course – Watt Light House, down at Watt Section by the old place." She always spoke of the cottage, built on Sheet Harbour Passage as 'the old place.' Actually, the cottage was built after the fire of the Show House, which was built by her husband Alexander. What a grand house it was. Everyone came from miles around to see it. However, this was after the fire, and Grammy brought up her whole family in the old place by the sea. Now, however, Grammy lived in the middle of the village of Sheet Harbour. A little abandoned fish and chip shop was made into a home for her. It was just on the other side of the driveway of her son Gerald and his wife Pearl. They could watch over her since she was in her later years.

"The Nova Scotia Government sent me a cheque once a month," Grammy continued. "It wasn't much mind you for all the work it took. Every evening just at dusk, I would take fire from the wood stove in my kitchen and walk across the field towards the lighthouse. It didn't matter whether it was raining or snowing. I didn't mind, for the beautiful evenings watching the sun setting made up for all the bad weather. More than once, I had a dickens of a time keeping my fire from going out before reaching the lighthouse. Then I had to return to the kitchen to get more fire from that wood stove. And when I got back to the lighthouse, I had to climb the ladder to the massive light. However, when I lit it – well it made my heart sing. I thought I was lighting up the whole world. I would think – there now – all the ships can see their way into the entrance of Sheet Harbour Passage and then up the mouth of Sheet Harbour. 'Watch out!' the light would say. 'Stay away from the rocks.' "

Bang, bang. It wasn't very loud, but loud enough to bring us back to the present. Then bang, bang. It was louder this time. Someone was knocking at the front door. The door was right there in her living room. But the front door was never used. My dad, my mom, and all other family members I ever knew used the back door. I don't think I ever came through the front door.

Bang, bang. My grandmother went to the window and slightly moved the curtain to see who was there. Then, using a hand motion, she ordered me to be quiet and stay put. I don't know how I knew I was to stay quiet, but I did.

Grammy's finger went to her lips, "Shhh! Shh! Be really quiet and she will go away."

I was straining my eyes to see out the parted curtains. All I could see was an old lady bent over, carrying a worn black cane. She was wearing a full-length dark coat, which may have been dark green at one time. It was too long for her; the bottom of her coat was dirty from dragging on the ground. I really thought this was odd because it was a beautiful summer morning. I was wearing yellow shorts and a matching short sleeve top with a sunflower on it.

Actually, she scared me. In my eyes, she looked like the wicked witch in the movie Snow White. Who was she and why didn't Grammy open the door? It wasn't like her to be unfriendly.

Finally, we watched as the old lady turned around and shuffled her way slowly out of the yard. After each step, she placed her cane down first and her feet slowly followed.

When I thought it safe to speak, I had to ask, "Who was she?"

"Oh, don't worry," my grandmother said, "it was just Maude. The last time I let her in, she just took her hands and fondled my best fern. She kept saying how beautiful, how beautiful, and do you know what happened? One week later that fern died. I don't let her in anymore!"

*****

"Sweetheart, are you alright? You look like you are in a world of your own." Paul was out of his swivel office chair and sitting next to me.

The room wasn't spinning any longer. The pictures of Peggy's Cove Lighthouse were in their places. Here Paul was looking worried and sitting beside me.

"Are you alright, dear?"

"Yes, I think so. Paul, I just had a flashback to my early childhood. I only met Maude once, if you can call it a meeting. My grandmother was not friendly towards her at all. Why would my grandmother not want to visit with her own sister? Show me more." I was up on my feet heading for the computer.

"I guess supper is going to be late." Paul drew up a chair and joined me.

"Well, you're the one who started this." The gold tea towel hit him on top of his head. Removing the towel with a smile, he placed his chair closer to the computer with mine.

"Who did Maude marry?" I was getting into this now.

"Looks like both your grandmother, Catherine and her sister Maude married Kenneys. Catherine married Alexander Kenney, and Maude married John Winslow Kenney.

"How was Alexander related to John Winslow?"

"They had the same grandfather Isaac. However, Isaac married twice, and John Winslow was from the second marriage. That makes them cousins."

"Who were Maude's children? How many did she have?"

"Well, let's see. According to this, her children were Kathleen Maud, Roy, Laurie, Harry, Pearl, Violet Matilda, Jean, and Frances Belle."

"You've got to be kidding me!"

"You're not going to faint again, are you?"

"No, and I didn't faint. But it can't be! Grammy made a big deal of it. She told us to stay away from Roy and Laurie Kenney and their families. We were to have nothing to do with them."

"Why?"

"She said because we weren't related and that they were trash."

"Now mind you, Roy owned and operated a pool hall. His wife Fran helped him. She worked behind the counter. They had a daughter younger than I; her name was Cathy. There were two of us. Two Cathy Kenneys. We used to get mail mixed up. Anyway, I would go there and Fran would have me sit at the counter with her Cathy, and she would give us candy. Grammy didn't know and would have had a fit if she had known. Laurie ran a dance hall. I was too young at the time to ever go there, but my sisters, Lois and Marlane, and my brothers, Barry and Wade, did go. Years later, when my parents retired in Sheet Harbour, my younger brothers, Blair and Darren, went as well."

"Did your grandmother know your sisters and brothers went?"

"I have no idea, but I assume she wouldn't like it."

"I have to call Barry. He's not going to believe this."

"Can't we eat first? I am starving."

*****

Barry was my older brother. He was third in line; Lois came first, then Marlane and Barry. Wade came next and then me. Two younger brothers, Blair and Darren, completed the family. You couldn't say you were lonely in my family, since there was always someone around.

"Hello, Barry."

"Well, hello, Cathy, how are you?"

Family members and anyone living in Canada called me Cathy. When I married Paul and we moved to the United States, I changed my name back to Catherine, for that was the name given to me at birth, and my parents called me Catherine. To this day, if someone calls me, Cathy, I know they are from Canada.

It was always nice to talk to my older brother Barry. Maybe he never realized how special an older brother was.

"Fine," I answered. "How is Cape Breton these days?"

"I'm not in Cape Breton. Too cold. Gail and I are in North Carolina. It's not cold here, just right."

"Playing any golf?"

"You know me, I play almost every day."

"I'm glad to hear that, for you wouldn't be playing golf this time of the year in Cape Breton, Nova Scotia. Shoveling snow, maybe, but not golf. I guess you know I'm doing research for my next book."

"Yes, and how is your first book The Lady Catherine book going?"

"Great. We're selling hundreds of that book now. The reason I'm calling, Barry, is that I've found something very interesting. Do you remember Roy and Laurie Kenney from Sheet Harbour?"

"Yes, they ran the pool hall and the dance hall as I recall. Hung out at the pool hall all the time. Summer memories."

"Do you also remember Grammy telling us we weren't related, even though they too were Kenneys?"

"Yes, she told us to stay away. Not that I ever did. Stay away that is."

"Well, do you know who Maude Kenney is?"

"No, I don't think so."

"Maude was Roy and Laurie's mother. Plus, I found out that Maude had a sister. Want to guess who?"

"Can't imagine. Who?"

"Grammy."

"Grammy, our Grammy? Wait a minute, did you say Grammy's sister is Maude and Maude's sons are Roy and Laurie?"

"That's right."

"Wow. You're kidding me?"

"That's what I said."

"I can't imagine what happened between Grammy and her sister. There must have been some kind of split. I'm going to try to find out."

"How are you going to do that?"

"I don't know yet, but I'll figure something out."

"If I know you – you'll sort all this out. Good luck and keep me posted."

"I will."

*****

Paul and I were washing dishes after the late dinner we had together. Scraping a plate, I handed it to him to place in the dishwasher. "This has been quite the day. I still can't help wondering what happened between Catherine and Maude to make such a split in the Kenney family. It's sad too."

"How is that?" Paul placed silverware in the plastic rack.

"I always thought I was special since I was named after Grammy Kenney."

"Yes, two Catherines in this conversation do make it tricky."

"What's so sad is I have no idea who Maude's side of the family is. They would be my cousins, wouldn't they?"

Closing the door of the dishwasher, Paul looked up at me. "Yes, they'd be your cousins. Now, what are you going to do about all of this?"

"What can I do about it?"

"I'm sure you'll think of something."

"I feel like Maude is calling out to me. I don't know what she is saying, but she is calling out to me."

I was not much company that evening. All I could think about was Maude. I really felt like she was calling out to me. I had so many questions. How do I find the answers?

Paul had returned to the TV room where he always went to study. I don't know why we called it the TV room, for we didn't watch TV except for the news. Paul looked up from the book he was reading. "Dear, have you figured out what you're going to do?"

"I guess I have to start somewhere."

"And where is that?"

"I'm going to contact the older cousins."

"Older cousins?"

"Yes, in my family there are older cousins and younger cousins. We have a very large family"

"And which group are you in? The older or younger, I mean?"

"Younger cousins. My father's parents, Catherine and Alexander, had twelve children. The older children married and had children of their own before my father and mother even met, let alone married with children. The older cousins are twenty-five and thirty years older than I am. They would not even recognize me if we passed each other on the street. I'm going to start there. Ask the older cousins if their parents ever spoke of an Aunt Maude. I don't remember my father ever talking about his Aunt Maude."

"When are you going to start?"

"Tomorrow sounds good to me."

Using the Gmail telephone on my computer, I contacted three of my father's nieces. I remember Aunt Hazel my father's sister and her husband, Uncle Oicle, well. I believe

Hazel was one of my father's favorite sisters. Mom and Dad would take my brother Blair and me to visit when we spent the summers in Sheet Harbour. By this time, Hazel and the Oicle children were all grown and didn't live at home any longer. I remember seeing Elry, their youngest son, but I don't remember ever seeing any of their other children. This is when I was ten years old, and, at that time, I didn't even know they had other children. The first phone call I made was to their daughter Gail.

Every time I dial a number to Nova Scotia, a feeling of excitement bubbles up from inside. I'm going to be talking to someone from home. Really, it doesn't matter if I'm related or not. I could be calling a bank and the feeling would be the same. I'm going to be talking to someone from my home. Nova Scotia will always be home.

I placed the numbers into the computer, and after a short time, I could hear ringing on the other end. Indiana calling Nova Scotia, it sure is a small world. After the third ring, I hear a "hello."

"Hello," I replied, "is this Gail?"

"Yes."

"My name is Catherine Wilcoxson. You would know me as Cathy Kenney, my maiden name. My father's name was Elbridge Kenney, and my mother was Doris."

"Of course, Elbridge Kenney. And you were one of the youngest. Yes, Cathy, I remember you. You were a quiet little girl with very blond hair."

"That was me."

"Where are you calling from?"

"Covington, Indiana. My husband, Paul, and I have lived here for five years now."

"All the way from Indiana. My, my and your mother, Doris, yes, Aunt Doris. She was always dressed perfectly and she was pretty too. She had beautiful dark hair and she was very kind. How is your mother?"

"She is fine. She lives in Northwood Towers on Gottingen Street in Halifax. She feels at home there at the nursing home. She has lived there for several years now."

"It's just so good to talk to you, Cathy. How are your sister Lois and your brothers?"

"Fine. Lois lives in Dartmouth, Barry in Cape Breton and Darren in Halifax. Darren gets to see Mother often."

"Cathy, I just want you to know that I loved reading your book. Remember, I bought several from you the last time you were here in Sheet Harbour. You had a table set up in Gammons' Hardware Store parking lot. Everyone was talking about you that weekend. I sent your book to my sister in Ontario, and she loved it too. Everyone liked your story about Captain Heman Kenney and his schooner the *Lady Catherine*. You know he was our great grandfather."

"Yes, I know. Thank you, I am glad you enjoyed the story. One reason I'm calling you is that I have a few questions about the family because I'm working on another book."

"Well, I don't know if I can answer them, but I'll try."

"I'm looking for any information about your mother's and my father's Aunt Maude."

"Aunt Maude, you say? Well, I don't know very much at all about Aunt Maude. I only saw her a few times, and I only remember Mother speaking about her occasionally. Come to think about it, we didn't have any contact with her when I was growing up."

"She would have been Grammy's sister."

"That's right, Grammy's sister."

"Do you think there was some kind of falling out between them?"

"I don't know. Maybe my sister would know more."

"Grammy told us we were not related to the other Kenneys there in Sheet Harbour. Except, I've recently found a connection between them."

"You need to call Carol Ann Owen. She is a friend and knows all the family trees of everyone in Sheet Harbour and there around, including all the Kenneys."

"I will. And thanks for talking to me, I have really enjoyed it."

"Now you call me and tell me everything you have heard. I'll also be talking to Carol Ann."

"Yes, I'll call you if I find out anything interesting. Thanks again for talking with me; you have a good evening. Goodbye."

"Goodbye, Cathy."

Therefore, my research into finding out about Maude began. My cousins didn't know very much about their mothers', Aunt Maude. Only that she was mentioned occasionally.

I did call Carol Ann Owen in Sheet Harbour. Turns out, she was my second cousin. Carol Ann did family trees for those living in Sheet Harbour.

She told me that Catherine, my grandmother, and Maude had an adopted brother named Edward. She couldn't tell me why Maude and Catherine never spoke. I didn't know my dad had an Uncle Edward. This was news to me. I had to find out more. I immediately called my mother.

I loved calling and talking to my mother. It was hard living so far away. We talked often and she was glad that I called. After asking how Mom was and exchanging the subject of weather, which happened to be sunny but cold, I finally got to the question that was really on my mind.

"Mom, did you know Daddy had an Uncle Edward?"

"No, Daddy did not have an Uncle Edward. At least not that I ever knew about. I think that if he had an Uncle Edward, I would have known about it."

"Did you know about Aunt Maude, Grammy's sister?"

"Yes, I remember them speaking about her now and then, but I never met her."

"Well, I just found out that Grammy and Maude had an adopted younger brother named Edward. Their parents, Ed and Flo Cook, adopted Edward when Grammy and Maude were quite young.

"How do you know this?"

"First, I called and talked to Gail?

"You did? And how is Gail? I haven't seen or spoken to her in years."

"Gail sends her greetings. In fact, she spoke of you with fond memories. She thought you were kind." Mother laughed.

"I'm not sure Gail knew about Edward; she didn't speak of him, but she told me to call a Carol Anne Owen from Sheet Harbour who has the family tree. When I was speaking with her on the phone, she read from the information she had researched about the Kenney family. She found government census that the Cook family adopted a baby boy shortly after his birth in 1893."

"I am fairly sure that your dad did not know of Edward, for he never spoke of him."

After telling Mom, I loved her and saying goodbye, I just sat in my chair staring into space.

Paul entered my office. "Are you still on the computer? Who are you talking to now?"

"I'm finished for the night. I was talking with Mom."

"Does she know anything about Edward?"

"Not a thing. Isn't that amazing? No one knows about Edward, except that he is listed in the government census as living with Grammy's parents, Ed and Flo. Edward is a real person whom no one knows. He was younger than Catherine and Maude."

"Come sit beside me, honey." Paul tapped the love seat he was sitting on. "I want to tell you what I found today."

"What have you found, dear?" I asked as I snuggled up beside him.

"A Ford Escape."

"A what?" I snuggled closer beside him on the love seat."

"You know we will need a vehicle to tow something on our trip."

Paul and I have been talking a lot about his retirement. A trip was on the top of the list.

"We don't have anything to tow."

"Not yet."

"I stopped at the Ford Dealer just for fun. They have this Ford Escape; I think you need to go see it. I will retire in nine months, and we're thinking about our trip to Nova Scotia."

"Yes, I'm working on a book tour, but there is still a lot of work to do on that."

The next day I found myself sitting inside a 2009 Ford Escape. It had all the bells and whistles you would ever want. It was silver-coloured and sparkled in the sunlight. There was a skylight, no hands held phone system, ambient lighting in four different colours, and, of course, a stereo system to play all of our CDs. In addition, Paul reminded me it would pull a small camper.

"Is this a car or truck? I asked."

"I've heard some call it a truck."

"I don't want a truck."

"Then, dear, let's call it a car/truck."

"Okay, a car/truck it will be. I tell you what." I looked over at him sitting on the passenger seat. "You buy this and I'll buy the camper."

He smiled, "What kind of camper?"

"The kind they call a popup camper. I don't want a big one, not that we can afford one."

"Are you sure you want to use your money?"

"Our money. Yes, I'm sure. My book is selling well and money in the bank. I think there's enough to buy a popup camper."

Two weeks later, we had a popup camper. In fact, we were trying to put it up in the backyard. You have to remember, the last time we put up a camper like this, our daughter, Jennifer, wasn't even in school yet. Today, she has her own children that age.

It took a while, and after several tries, we finally managed to get it up. We stood back and looked at each other with a big grin. "Now we're ready."

"Nine months to go and then retirement." Paul was looking at me. "I think I'll be ready."

*****

Sitting on folding canvas camping chairs, we couldn't take our eyes away from the beautiful view. The afternoon sunlight was shining through the yellow and orange leaves of two giant maple trees. The only sound one could hear was the gentle breeze blowing the leaves from the tree, making them float to join the others, as they piled up around our camper.

"You know it's always sad."

"What is sad?" Paul turned and looked at me.

"All the leaves are falling. A sign that summer is really over. Winter will be here before you know it."

"Now winter makes me sad, that's for sure."

I had to laugh at him. "Silly, not that it's going to be cold; that's not what makes me sad. It's the only season where you can see the end. The end of spring you don't even notice changing into summer. However, when fall comes, everything changes. It gets colder, the leaves fall off the trees, and kids go back to school."

"We don't have any kids to go back to school."

"Don't remind me of our empty nest, dear. However, someones' kids are going back to school. It was always sad to see the end of summer and the beginning of fall. Here we are in the fall in Indiana; it has warm days and cool nights. Just right for camping. We're testing out this camper, for after all, if we're going from Indiana to Nova Scotia for three months, we have to make sure we can do this."

"That's right." My mood changed to excitement. "We're going to have a great adventure, aren't we?"

"I think we will have an adventure for sure," Paul answered.

"I think it will be fun; we like camping. Sure, we haven't done it in years, but you see how fast it comes back. Like riding a bike, once you learn you never forget. Plus, I'll be able to do more research about Maude. You know, Paul, she is still calling me."

Paul put his arm around me. "It's a story that needs an ending, and who would be the most perfect to figure it out than you? But right now let's roast some of those marshmallows."

The camper was stored in the garage for the winter. The garage was just big enough to fit both the camper and the car/truck. Every time we got into the car/truck we could see the camper, which was a reminder that winter would end and camping would begin sometime in the spring. In addition, our great adventure would start.

During the months of February and March, I was able to set up the book tour in Nova Scotia. The calendar started to fill up. I was invited to every summer festival in Nova Scotia.

While the snow flew and the winds howled, I talked to Gail and Carol Ann. They looked forward to me being with them in person in Sheet Harbour the last week of June. Maude is still calling and the research will continue.

Chapter Two

Free at Last – Free at Last– Retirement

This may be a slight exaggeration. It was much more serious when Martin Luther King cried, "Free at last, free at last, Thank God almighty, we are free at last..." How many times in your life do you feel free? Maybe it begins when you graduate from high school, and you are on your way to college. Maybe it is when your last child goes to kindergarten. My daughter says you yell, "Free at last – Free at last."

Paul has always loved his job. Being a minister for 42 years brings many rewards. However, being ready to serve day and night can wear a person out. Therefore, I asked him, "Paul, what would be the perfect retirement?"

"The perfect retirement you ask, well, first I would not give up preaching, and teaching about Jesus; that will continue all of my life. It would be nice not to have to run a church – alone I mean. Making bulletins, dealing with people, sometimes it is easier to work with animals. Sometimes I felt as if people brought me out once or twice a week, put me in front of the congregation, and then put me back on the shelf when they didn't need me. It can get pretty lonely, you know."

"With retirement, how will that change?" I asked.

"We can go and do what we want to do when we want to do it. No one can tell us it's time to move on. I am looking forward to the freedom. I still want to be a servant of Christ. He will find me places to preach. In the meantime, I'll fix computers, and you'll write books. We've prepared for this retirement. I took that course on computers, and we bought our retirement home in DeQuincy two years ago."

Of course, DeQuincy, Louisiana, the place where we spend most of our off time. We had lived there for several years, working with the church. When we moved on, we left Jennifer, our daughter, and Michael, her husband, and our grandsons to fend for themselves. We visit them and the church twice a year. DeQuincy looked like the retirement place. Christmas vacation two years ago we found a house. It was in pretty bad shape, but I could see the potential. The backyard was wonderful if you could see 'wonderful' through the tall grass and several wire link fences. The last owner must have kept more than one dog out there. However, what you could see through all of the mess were two giant live oak trees. They made an umbrella over the half acre of the backyard. I have always been a tree person and these trees were just beautiful. They were hundreds of years old, and you had to wonder who else in times past sat under the shade of these trees. There was a small deck to sit on just outside the back door. The house had good bones. So we bought it and painted the whole inside, making it livable, allowing us to rent it out for two years.

My mind went back to retirement and Paul continued. "We have saved the rent money and now we have the money to renovate it. In addition, our trip of a lifetime will begin the next day after I retire. Then, of course, research; now we'll have time for research. Maude may be calling you, but I kind of wonder what happened to her myself."

"The trip of a lifetime. It's all set. We have to be in Mill Village, Shubenacadie, Nova Scotia on June 10, 2012."

Meantime, in April, our friends from Orchard Hills church helped load our furniture in a Penske moving truck, and we took it to DeQuincy, Louisiana. What were we going to do with all of our household belongings? We certainly couldn't take it with us on our trip in June. The answer was to put it in a truck and take it to Louisiana.

Paul was the truck driver and I was the co-pilot. I was always thankful that Paul grew up a farm boy. He could drive anything. He was in the army before I ever met him. In the army, he drove tanks. Every move we made, and there were more than eight of them, Paul drove the moving truck. Furthermore, I might add, he did it very well.

Now we're not spring chickens anymore. You have no idea how many stares we received at every truck stop we arrived at. Here came this old couple with a truckload of a lifetime of collecting stuff. Just to get in and out of the truck was a chore. The truck drivers who do this for a living were very kind to us. They would open doors for me as I entered the gas station and ask, "Are you okay?" I would reply, "Just fine, thank you" and give him a big smile.

When we arrived in DeQuincy, Paul handed the keys to the truck to our son-in-law, Michael, and said, "You can drive it to the house."

Our retirement house was still rented. However, we had outbuildings on the property. Paul planned to set up his computer business in one of the buildings. But for now, the building would make a great place to store all of our belongings. Jennifer, Michael, and other friends of ours emptied the truck and filled the building to the top.

We enjoyed visiting grandsons, Logan, Ethan, and Connor. However, we weren't finished with Indiana yet. So we headed back to Covington, Indiana.

The house was now empty. For a month, all we had was a bed and camping equipment for the trip. The camping chairs were set up to watch a very small TV, which just fit in the camper.

Sunday, May 27, 2012, the day we have planned for five years. Everything is packed. The car/truck is packed. Everything in its place. We even have a car top carrier, which we have named 'the hamburger,' on the roof. The name 'hamburger' came from Michael our-son-in law many years ago. Before Jennifer and he were married, we took a road trip from Maryland to Ontario, Canada. We had one of these carriers on the top of the car, and Michael said it looked like a hamburger.

 We spent the last few days packing and repacking. Saying our goodbyes to very good friends.

Paul's last sermon in Indiana was "Farewell to Orchard Hills."

The church here has been very good to us. We will miss the people. Nevertheless, a new chapter of our lives begins today.

After church services, a special farewell luncheon was given to us. With a homemade retirement cake and all. Then they gathered around our car/truck and waved farewell. It was almost as if we had just gotten married. I looked at Paul, and we smiled as we started our retirement together.

"One more stop before the trip of a lifetime."

"Yes, just one more stop, Cincinnati."

Cincinnati to say goodbye to Christopher our son, his wife Kayla, and our granddaughter Lily. I was deep in thought for a while. There were many things to think about. One was not seeing Christopher and his family. "Paul, you know we're just making a tradeoff today."

"Yes, I'm aware that we are. We won't see Christopher, Kayla, and Lily every month. Now, after our trip, we will see Jennifer, Michael, and the boys. Life isn't perfect, dear. We will just have to make the best of things."

"Do you feel free?"

"I feel something that is new, and the feeling is one that I could get used to." We journeyed along on the familiar highway to see Christopher. We had made this trip many times, and this would be the last. Our son was waiting for us as we drove into his driveway.

"Do we look any different?" I asked, as I reached out and hugged him.

"Yes, I believe you do. I can't put my finger on it exactly, but something about your eyes."

"That's a good one, son." Paul gave his son a hug.

"Well, she asked," he chuckled. "Come on in the house; Lily is waiting for you."

We hugged and played and hugged and played some more with Lily. Grandchildren are wonderful. Lily will be two in July. I won't be here. It's going to be hard to make the best of it.

The very first time to put the camper up was in Christopher's driveway. It took us a while and even had to have help from his neighbour. I think Christopher began to worry about us and the trip we were going on. We were ready to plug into the electricity from the house. When we did, it blew all the fuses. Our air conditioner drew too much power. Oh, well, we'll do without it. It was a hot night sleeping.

*****

Our trip from Ohio to Maine was most enjoyable. The scenery of mountains and the white clouds in the blue sky made the time pass quickly. We stopped at a campground for two nights. We had the place mainly to ourselves, for schools were not out for summer vacation yet. Beautiful mountains of Pennsylvania all around.

The day we crossed the border to Canada was a happy one for me. We stopped to buy supplies in Woodstock, Maine, for I remembered once we cross the border, there was a lot of open country or wilderness as far as you could see.

Just before sunset in New Brunswick, we saw a sign for camping. It was time to stop; we were ready to put the camper up and go to bed. However, our camper decided to give us trouble. As we pulled the bed compartment out, it broke. Panic was beginning to creep in, but before it could take over, out of nowhere, an older man walked up and asked how we were. Other than having no place to sleep, fine I thought. He noticed right away what the problem was and said, "Not to worry; my son is working in a machine shop right over there, and he can make you a metal part that is needed for your bed."

We had prayed for God to watch over us and now He has sent us an angel. He just came from nowhere.

Now, folks, it didn't take us long to accept the offer. Thanks to the work of those nice angels, it wasn't long before we were tucked into our bed and counting sheep. Thank you, Lord.

The next morning, Paul and I took a walk down by the lake, which was tucked in between the rolling hills, giving the impression of large rolls of green carpet running into the water. Everything was green, and the sky was blue with just a few fluffy white clouds floating by. It really felt like spring. I was expecting cold and rain, but this was the earliest I had seen spring come to this part of Canada. I was prepared for warm camping coats for both Paul and me. The

June weather we were having was more like July. We hardly ever used our coats. We actually put them in the hamburger, and that's where they stayed until fall.

When we arrived in Mill Village and turned into the driveway of the Church of Christ, a feeling of happiness gushed from my heart. The same feeling I got at the border crossing into Nova Scotia. The happiness was spilling, and I couldn't help smiling. "We're here, dear, I can't believe it, but we're here. Our home base for the whole summer, right in the backyard of this church building." It was a lovely place to set up our campsite. And there came Joan Mackey, our first visitor.

It's no wonder we feel at home in Mill Village, since we lived here for seven years. Our daughter Jennifer was born here. We have kept in touch with these lovely people and now we're back.

Our adventure is upon us. We're here to promote my book, *The Adventures of Captain Heman Kenney and Lady Catherine - 1833-1917*. A Nova Scotia story of a schooner captain, his love for his schooner *Lady Catherine,* and the love of his life, Elizabeth. Most authors would call this trip, a book tour.

Another reason we're here is to find out about Maude. We plan to get answers to the many questions we have about her. In addition, Paul will be preaching sermons on Sunday mornings to the people we love in Mill Village.

Our first place to go was Sheet Harbour. We arrived in Sheet Harbour on June 11. Crossing the bridge over Malay Falls, we could see the harbour; I had almost forgotten how pretty it was. The clear water from West River was tumbling over rocks and down the hill, where the water spills into Sheet Harbour. I opened my window to hear the roar of the water passing under the bridge as we drove over it. So many memories filled my mind and my heart. I spent my summers here as a child. My parents brought the children to the cabin right on the harbour. My father made a beach where we could swim when the tide was high. In later years, my father retired here. Many of my relatives chose Sheet Harbour as home. Catherine, my grandmother, and her sister, Maude, whom I did not know, lived most of their lives here. We arranged to park our camper in Cecil Kenney's yard, and it turned into a nice visit.

As we turned into his laneway, Paul asked, "Is he an older cousin or a younger cousin?"

"Cecil is an older cousin. I don't think he even remembers me being around. However, I remember him and his brother Eric well. I was amazed at some of the wild things they did. They were older teenagers and I was but seven or eight. Cecil and his brother came down to our cabin to visit. They walked out to the point, which was a grassy ridge right on the harbour. They had a bag of 45-RPM records. They took each record and skipped it across the water as if you would a flat stone. After they tired of that, they took off their shirts and dove into the water for a swim. Being a young girl, I was amazed."

My book tour would begin here in Sheet Harbour. A fitting place, considering Sheet Harbour and Watt Section were the main backdrops of my book about Captain Heman Kenney and his schooner, *Lady Catherine.*

Tuesday morning at 8 a.m., Paul drove us to the Duncan MacMillan High School. It was a beautiful spring morning; the sun was shining, making its light shimmer off the blue water of the harbour. "You know, Paul, this is the school my brothers Blair and Darren attended after Dad retired and moved here to Sheet Harbour. I've never been inside. I know they bus the kids here for miles on either side of Sheet Harbour."

"It's a nice size high school in a small community." We turned off Number 7 Highway and continued up the hill. We were headed into the forest. I turned around and looked back down from where we came. We could see East River flowing towards and passing the government wharf and then out into Eastern Passage, where it would empty into the Atlantic Ocean. I had forgotten how the colour blue was so vibrant in Nova Scotia. The water in the harbour was a gorgeous blue, the river water was a lighter blue, and the sky was blue, blue, blue. No wonder my favorite colour is blue. The water off the government wharf was very deep. Large schooners could dock there and disembark all their wares. Even the famous schooner the *Bluenose,* an ambassador for the Maritimes, had docked there. The Maritimes are the provinces of Nova Scotia, New Brunswick, Prince Edward Island, Newfoundland, and Labrador. The *Bluenose* was famous all over Canada, for her image was engraved upon the Canadian dime. She would sail wherever the ocean wind took her, to foreign ports, where her crew would tell stories and customs of Nova Scotia.

"Paul, did you see that government wharf that we just passed? There is very deep water off that wharf, and believe it or not, as kids we would jump off the wharf and swim."

We entered the schoolyard. There were several giant potholes filled with water. Paul carefully drove around them to find a place to park. "Talking about swimming, maybe you could do so in that pothole over there." We both had a good laugh.

Figure 3: Visiting with my mother, Doris, admiring my quilt

Figure 4: Outside library talking about Maude and Edward to "older cousins."

Figure 5: The Maritime Museum of the Atlantic did a book launch for Catherine.

Figure 6: Our camper parked at our home base, Mill Village Church, Shubenacadie, Nova Scotia

"Must have had rain here recently." I opened the back hatch of the car/truck. Paul took a box of my books; I took my binder with all my notes in it. "I don't remember it being this nice in June, Paul, just look around at everything blooming." Yellow dandelions were everywhere. The tulips and daffodils were finished; they were standing in a garden by the flagpole, naked and waiting for the next spring. In big letters read Duncan MacMillan High School, Home of the Eagles.

Figure 7: Me with tall ships in background, Halifax Harbour

Figure 8: The pirates followed us all over Nova Scotia.

Figure 9: Is that Jack Sparrow?

Figure 10: Davy Jones

Figure 11: View of wharf in Lunenburg

Figure 12: Sailors marching on wharf in Halifax

Figure 13: Selling my book. Digby Harbour.

Figure 14: Liverpool, Nova Scotia.

Figure 15: St. Peter's, Cape Breton

Figure 16: Tent tied to an anchor, Lunenburg

Figure 17: Set up at county fair in Antigonish

Figure 18: Library in Digby, just one of my book presentations

Figure 19: On our way home to Louisiana

Figure 20: The *Bounty* sank in a Hurricane off North Carolina, shortly after we returned to Louisiana.

The entrance to the school had a wall of typical cement blocks, which were arranged in an artful way. We could see right through some of them. The double doors opened to a large stair landing. A very wide staircase of a dozen steps or more was right in front of us. To our left, the stairs continued up to the second floor. We had to make a decision to go up or down. We decided to go down. The stairs going down led to a wide hallway with doors to offices. Picking the door that had a sign Principal's Office, we went inside. Every principal's office looks the same. A very high counter stretched from one wall to the other, making standing a good way to communicate. There were a few students in line before us, so waiting our turn gave me a chance to look around. On the wall was a picture of Queen Elizabeth of England. Her picture always reminded me of my mother. They were about the same age, and I thought the queen looked like my mother. Pictures of student activities were crowded on the other wall. Hockey teams, girls and boys, basketball, track and field, and speech club. They all made me smile, for my thoughts were: *Oh to be young again.*

When it was our turn, I looked towards the lady in front of me. "I believe Molly Gammon is expecting me." The secretary smiled when she heard my name. She informed us she would tell Molly we were here. We sat down, Paul with the box of books and me with my folder.

Entering Molly's office, I could tell by the look on her face, she was expecting someone different from me. "Welcome," she finally smiled. I wondered what she was expecting. Maybe someone a lot younger.

I handed her a book. My book, *The Adventures of Captain Heman Kenney and Lady Catherine - 1833-1917*. As she looked at the book, I enthusiastically made the comment, "A book written about Sheet Harbour. Isn't that amazing? Who knew someone would write a book about Sheet Harbour."

"That's amazing," she replied as she studied the book.

"I'm beginning a book tour of Nova Scotia. What a better place to start than the very setting of the book."

"We're looking forward to you speaking to the grade sevens and grade eights. I've reserved the library for you to do the presentations."

"That sounds fine," I replied.

"Maybe I need to make it clear to you that these students may be a little unruly at times."

I'm sure she was a little worried about me, this old lady. I might be eaten up by those students. "I'm sure I'll be fine," I assured her. After my presentation, I'll be asking if they have any questions."

"They may not ask questions, and to tell you the truth, I'm afraid they may give you a hard time throughout your presentation."

"I'm sure I'll be fine," I reassured her.

"Nevertheless," Molly said, "I'll feel better if two of the teachers, better still four of them, stay with you. They will be helpful if you have any problems."

"That will be all right having the four teachers there. They will not bother me at all."

Molly then showed us the direction to the library. "Stop into the office before you leave. I want to make sure the school buys several copies of your book."

Molly didn't have to worry about me and the junior high students. I had more experience than she knew. While living in Jena, Louisiana, and Covington, Indiana, I was a substitute teacher at every level of schools, including Middle School, which was called Junior High in Canada, and in the High Schools. For years, I have been teaching Bible classes to every age from adults to very young children. Therefore, I had no fear.

Paul and I had a few minutes before grade seven classes filed into the library, and behind them, came four teachers. I hadn't been speaking very long before I had them eating out of the palm of my hand so to speak. Not only were the students with me on every word I spoke, but also the teachers. The questions I asked at the end had very interesting answers. Questions like how long it took me to write the book and did Captain Heman Kenny really live here? I love working with this age group.

Grade eights were a little more challenging, but it didn't take them long to be drawn into my stories. The questions at the end were going nowhere. They seemed to think it was beneath them to answer anything I asked, until I exclaimed, "Come on, you guys. Grade seven knew all the answers to my questions. You don't want them to find out that you couldn't answer my questions, do you?"

Immediately the atmosphere changed and we had a lively discussion. When the bell rang, several students came up to me to ask more about the book. I thought it went well. In addition, there were several Kenneys in the class; those students were related to me.

The teachers were amazed. They hadn't seen their students so eager to please in a long time. One teacher came to me and said he loved my presentation. However, I had several errors about the history of Sheet Harbour. I write of a Pulp Mill being in West River. That's where it was ever since I was a child. However, he informed me that the Pulp Mill I was writing about in the 1800's was located in West

River. I was happy to receive the correct information, for I had to rely on foggy memories I had as a child.

Another teacher came to me; she was planning to attend Mount Saint Vincent University that summer to work on her Master's Degree. She believed the professors at Mount Saint Vincent University in Halifax would be interested in hearing my presentation. And they did, for a little over three weeks later, I was presenting my book to her graduate class.

The high school bought several copies of my book for their library. This is not the first time I had been in Sheet Harbour to tell about my book. A year or so ago I spent a weekend here. I set up a table at Gammons Brothers' Hardware store. It was a lovely summer day. Word got around quickly, being a small town, that there was a lady selling a book in the parking lot of Gammons, and the book was about Sheet Harbour. My relatives, mainly the older cousins gathered around me. Some had to introduce themselves to me. Plus, the same weekend I had a table at a craft show. A crowd gathered around our table, for Paul had his computer and a genealogy program, which enabled him to tell how they were related to me. However, at that time, the school was not in session and the library was not open, causing them not to see my book. At that time, we did stop at the flower shop and asked if they wanted to sell it, which they did.

"How do you think my presentation went?" Paul and I were in the car/truck heading for the flower shop.

Paul smiled. "Never doubted you, my dear. Some others may have, but I knew you would have them as you say, eating out of your hand."

We turned into the driveway of the flower shop. "Let's go in and see how book sales are."

I was the first out of the car/truck, heading for the front entrance. The harbour was directly behind the flower shop. You could throw a rock and it would hit the water. The soft spring breeze slapped the blue water up on the shore. I took a deep breath of the salty air as I led us in through the open door. The sound of a bell announced our arrival. This flower shop was an old two-story white house with black trim. The upstairs was used as their living quarters. Downstairs in the main part of the house, there were three rooms. Two were turned into display areas with different kinds of tables displaying teacups, vases filled with flowers, wreaths decorated with colourful artificial flowers, and knickknacks of every kind. Among everything stood a copy of my book.

Vicky met us before we entered the back room. This is the room where she worked on flower orders for her faithful customers. Just make an order, and she would have a beautiful flower arrangement ready in no time.

"Nice to see you," she said. "Welcome back to Sheet Harbour. I have a cheque for you; we sold several of your books."

"It's always a pleasure to be back in Sheet Harbour, so many memories. My grandmother, Catherine, of course, is no longer here, but I can close my eyes and see her sitting in her rocking chair in her little cottage up the road. I'm afraid the cottage is gone as well. So is my Aunt Pearl's house. It was the meeting place in Sheet Harbour; there were always people stopping by."

"My mother's grandmother was Maude." Vicky was eager for me to know. "She was a Kenney, maybe some relation to Captain Heman Kenney in your book."

I couldn't believe my ears to hear the name, Maude. "I believe your mother's grandmother, Maude, and my grandmother, Catherine, were sisters. They both married Kenneys."

"How come they say we aren't related then? My husband and I spent many years in Ontario. We came back to Sheet Harbour just a few years ago, bought this house, and turned it into a flower shop. The first thing I was told was that my Kenneys and the other Kenneys were not related. But if your grandmother and my mother's grandmother were sisters, that certainly makes us related."

"It surely does. I'm doing research for another book while I'm here in Sheet Harbour. I need to know everything I can find about Maude Kenney, your mother's grandmother. Is it possible that I can visit with your mother? She could tell me everything she knows about Maude. Paul and I will be here in Sheet Harbour until Friday."

"Oh, I don't know, my mother is older now, and this has been a hard year for her. Several relatives have died, and I don't think she would have the time. Plus, I don't want her to think of the past right now."

"I wouldn't upset her. I would ask very positive questions."

"No, I don't think so."

Inside I was crying, *"Why, why?"* I would love to talk to her about Maude and the other side of the Kenneys. The side I don't know anything about. Nevertheless, it wasn't to be.

"Oh, Paul, why won't she let me meet her mother?" We were back in the car/truck heading for the Sheet Harbour Library.

"I don't know, but Vicky has made it clear that it's not going to happen."

"Maybe we will find something out at the library. Look, there is the library sign. Your name is not even on it. I wonder if they have done any advertising for your presentation on Thursday night."

The high school did a good job of making it known I was coming and why. The only sign of my presentation taking place on Thursday at the library was a little sign sitting on the front counter. If you didn't come into the library, you would never know. I had one day to spread the news, and I did. Any person I talked to I invited them to come, including a lady I met in the grocery store.

Meanwhile, we did research. Anything they knew about the Kenneys. The library had an old book written in 1954 by a Rutledge called *"Sheet Harbour, A Local History."* The ladies at the library suggested I contact Brady Josey, for he seemed to know who everyone was in Sheet Harbour and where they came from.

We left having an appointment to see Brady Josey at his house that very afternoon. I also checked out the book, *"Sheet Harbour, a Local History.* Of course, I didn't have a library card; the only reason they let me take the book was because I would be back in two days to give a presentation. The other reason was that every lady in the library knew Cecil, my cousin.

I sat at the little table in our camper, reading, and reading as fast as I could. So much information that I could use. As I was taking notes, Paul interrupted and said, "It's time to leave for our appointment with Brady Josey."

"Paul, I don't think I'm going to have the time to get all the information I need out of this book."

"All you can do is your best." He opened the car/truck door for me and I slid inside.

Meeting with Brady Josey was fascinating to me. He had my full attention from the time I walked into his home. He was ready for us. Pictures lay scattered on his kitchen table. He placed one picture before me and asked, "Do you know who these people are?"

"Oh my goodness," I replied and took a closer look. "That is my father, no, not my father; that is Alexander, my father's father. My father looked just like Alexander. There is my father, Elbridge. Paul, look how young he is, and he is all dressed up. They are all dressed up. Furthermore, his mother, Catherine, is right beside Alexander. Most of the family is here. Eda, Sadie, Betha, his sisters, and that man is Gerald his brother with his wife, Pearl."

"I didn't know all their names." Brady was pleased to get more information. "I have made a copy for you."

"Thank you; I have never seen this picture. I will cherish it always."

The rest of the visit was just as amazing. We found a lot of information about Maude and her family. Not only that, Brady knew about Edward and told us stories about him. He had two photocopies of the book from the library that I had been reading. He offered to sell it to me, but the cost was more than the cost of my own book. I didn't want to spend the money.

Our research about Maude continued. We left with advice to go to the Archives in Halifax, and he even gave us a contact who worked there. He invited us to come back that afternoon, and he would show us where Maude and Catherine lived as a child.

"Well, that was a productive morning." I sat down on my side of the table in the camper. I opened the book and continued to make notes.

Now it was Paul's turn to say it was a productive afternoon, scary but productive. Brady took us to the East River and to Cook Road. We were up at the top of Cook Road and in a driveway. Brady was pointing out where the house would have stood back in Maude and Catherine's day.

All of a sudden, a man came flying out of his back door, waving his arms and swearing words I hadn't heard spoken for many years. That fellow was not happy. Brady tried to talk to him.

"It's okay; I am showing this couple where the old Cook homestead used to be."

"You mean those Kenneys, don't you? Those no good blankety-blank Kenneys. All they want to do is take my land. I will shoot any Kenney, who sets foot on my property.

I leaned over to Brady. "Don't tell him I'm a Kenney."

"I think we had better leave." Brady looked concerned. "You can tell he has been drinking. I don't know what has gotten into him."

"Good idea; let's just leave." Paul was not happy about being there either.

No matter, I got the whole backdrop of my new book. Before we left, I decided to buy a copy of *"Sheet Harbour, A Local History;* I didn't have time to take notes, and I could certainly use the book. Things like how the mail was delivered back in the early 1900s and the description of Sheet Harbour at that time. In addition, the book mentioned Edward by name and the trouble he had made for himself. We thanked Brady for showing us everything.

About a dozen people came out to hear my presentation that Thursday evening at the library. Several of them were relatives that I had visited the day before. The lady I had met in the grocery store came. That was Elsie Beaver; we became friends. I'm sure, if the word had gotten out in the community, we would have had more people. I was a little disappointed, but it turned out to have a silver lining after all.

The older cousins Gail and Ada and my second cousin, Carol Ann, were there. After the presentation, we all stood out beside our cars and talked for a good hour.

I asked questions about Edward. I was aware that Carol Ann knew, for she is the one who told me about him. However, I had no idea whether Gail and Ada knew about Edward.

Ada began by saying, "We didn't talk about Edward. Our parents and grandparents didn't talk about him either."

Between the three ladies, I found out alarming and sad things about Edward. Back in his day, if there was trouble, it was never spoken of, and if it wasn't spoken of, it didn't happen.

I listened to both sides of the story. Maude's side was spoken by Carol Ann. Catherine's side was told by Gail and her sister Ada. Could this be where the split happened? I don't know for sure. The research would continue.

We headed back to Mill Village, Shubenacadie, our home base for the summer. Paul came from the States back in the 1970s to preach at the little church in Mill Village.

That is where I met the man from Tennessee. We married. That was 37 years, six states, and two provinces ago.

We set up the camper in the backyard of the church building. Sundays that we were here, Paul preached sermons to them. We love the people and it was like coming home.

The next week we headed for Liverpool. We were invited to make a presentation at their library during their summer festival 'Privateer Days'. We spent Canada Day there. We waved Canadian flags, which were flying everywhere. Watched parades with the Royal Canadian Mounted Police, the bagpipes, and a platoon of the British Army dressed in uniforms, as they would have appeared in the 1700 and 1800s. Americans would know them as the Red Coats. I was really enjoying being home.

I was treated as a celebrity right from the day we arrived. The organizers of this festival 'Privateer Days' set us up in a campground just outside the town. Then paid the bill. After setting up the camper, we had time for a walk. We could hear the waves of the ocean coming ashore, but we couldn't see the ocean through the trees. We walked to the small beach and not a person was there. Up the beach to the left were three boathouses. We headed up that way to explore. Pictures had to be taken of the quaint little cove. We sat and took in the quiet. Not completely quiet, for the seagulls were gliding through the sky calling to one another.

The next morning was such a pretty day. We set up our presentation tent where we sold books, placing small Canadian flags all around it. We had a visitor walk by our table. It was Jack Sparrow the pirate himself. He didn't seem to be a fellow to mess with, for he asked me, "What are you doing here, you wench? Go back to your ship." He did give me a hug and allowed Paul to take a picture of us. To this day, Paul laughs whenever he thinks about it. That afternoon we met several nice people at the library. Our close friend, George Mansfield, from Ontario, told his sister Bev we would be there. We ate fish and chips with them and enjoyed the company of her and her husband. Then, before we knew it, the weekend was over, and we headed back to Mill Village.

One of the highlights of our trip to Nova Scotia was to attend the "Tall Ships Festival" in Halifax. The last time we were in Halifax, the Maritime Museum of the Atlantic gave me a book launch. The trip that Paul and I will be on today is different because of the Tall Ship Festival. This festival celebrates the era of the sails or power from the wind. The era of the great schooners large and small. Different countries are invited to send a tall sailing ship to represent them. They're quite the sight to see when they sail into Halifax Harbour. Being a large harbour, the tall ships were able to come in with full sails. They make a pass around the harbour before they dock at the wharf, which extends along the waterfront of Halifax. Thousands of people come and buy tickets to go aboard the tall ships. There were at least 30 ships docked in the city of Halifax. One of the tall ships was the *HMS Bounty*, a half-century-old 180-foot long wooden sailing ship and quite a sight to see. Several months later, we were horrified to see on the news that she sank in Hurricane Sandy roughly 100 miles off Cape Hatteras, North Carolina. A deckhand, Claudene Christian, lost his life, and Captain Robin Walbridge went down with the ship. We had fond memories of seeing the *Bounty* in Halifax.

I was invited to return as a guest at the Maritime Museum. I was in their boathouse, right on the wharf of Halifax Harbour. This was the best place in all of Halifax. In fact, we were watching the nightly news at my sister's house in Dartmouth, where we were staying. The news stated the vendors along the waterfront complained that they had to pay $1000 to be able to sell during the Tall Ships Festival. This was double the price they paid during the regular summer tourist season.

My sister, Lois looked over to me and asked, "How much are you paying to be on the wharf?"

Paul and I looked at each other and said, "It's free. We are part of the museum; they have brought us in and it's free."

"How is it that the regular vendors have to pay double and more, and you're getting a place free?" Lois didn't understand how her little sister could do this.

"God takes good care of me." I smiled at Paul.

"I wouldn't go around telling people you got the place free." Keith my brother-in-law had good advice.

I had the best place on the whole downtown wharf. The boathouse had huge doors that opened towards the wharf. The boathouse was divided into two parts. Windows were used as the divider. You could stand at the windows and watch craftsmen build on a wooden schooner. Turning around, you could see two wooden schooners. They had steps you could climb to get to the top of the keel. What you don't see, when a sailboat or schooner is in the water, is a five to ten-ton keel that is under the water. This keeps them from tipping over. People would come in to see the schooners and the craftsman at work building a schooner. Paul and I were sitting there with my book. Thousands of people passed by. We were happy to be there for a week. We sold many books, and I had a chance to tell people about Halifax, my home.

Our old friend Jack Sparrow the pirate came to see us again. This time he brought with him his friends, Davy Jones and a number of other pirates.

To top it off, my mother lived ten minutes away at North Wood Nursing Home. At the end of the day, we would visit her. I would dump all the money I had made that day on her bed, and we would count it together.

After leaving Halifax, some of the Tall Ships followed the coastline of Nova Scotia, visiting the towns that had harbours that could accommodate the Tall Ships. Paul and I followed the Tall Ships down the coastline to Lunenburg. Of course, we had to take the roads, and, of course, our camper was pulled behind us.

Lunenburg is a fishing town built on the side of the bluff that rose from the harbour. You may enter a building in their front door on one street. Go up a set of stairs to the back door, which then opened onto another street that ran horizontally along the bluff. The connecting streets ran perpendicular and were definitely going uphill.

An interesting side note. For several years, a popular TV program titled *Haven* was filmed here in Lunenburg and other scenic parts of Nova Scotia. The town of Haven was told to be in Maine but actually was in Lunenburg, Nova Scotia. I would enjoy watching the program just to see pictures of home.

The Fisheries Museum of the Atlantic, on the wharf over the harbour, was waiting for us. All the buildings of the museum, boathouses, and warehouses along the small harbour were painted red.

This is the first time on our trip we ran into bad weather. It was raining and raining hard. It wasn't easy to find a parking place for our car/truck pulling a camper. When we finally made it inside the museum, we looked like drowned rats. Their Tall Ship Festival started the next day and we all hoped for the sunshine. We could come back in the morning and set up outside the museum.

The rain was still coming down with no let up in sight. Trying to find the campground in the rain was not a fun task. Then we had the hardest time setting up the camper. This was the first rain we had since the first of June, and we were now past the middle of July. Therefore, we tried not to be too discouraged when everything got wet.

The sun was shining the next morning as we headed back to the museum. Our tent was set up close to the front doors. The tent was pitched right over a very large black anchor. 'Large' isn't the word to use, since it weighed several tons. Our tent was tied to it, and for sure, it wasn't going anywhere, no matter how much the wind blew.

Here in Lunenburg, we sold every book we had. Paul quickly got on our computer and made a book order back to the States. We would be supplied with books in three days, not enough time to follow the Tall Ships to another town, so we headed back home to Mill Village.

Since we had a few days open, we went to Halifax for a day trip. The first thing we did was to knock on my brother Darren's door. He works nights, and he was just starting his day. We enjoyed having lunch with him. After lunch, we went to the Nova Scotia Archives. Maude was still calling. You had to sign in and have a special name tag to enter. We had to place all our belongings in a locker. I had to learn how to use the projector for microfilm. We had many people helping us because I believed they too heard Maude calling. What we found amazed us. I couldn't make up this stuff. Sometimes the historical stories are better than fiction. Now I understood better why my grandmother's family wouldn't talk about Edward. This must have been the rift that tore two sisters apart. It wasn't Maude, who had a problem, nor did Catherine; it was Edward. He was the one that tore the family to pieces.

What's sad to me is that this family thought they had put the whole thing behind them. Never again would they mention it. My father and mother didn't know about Edward. However, they had no idea that, in less than one hundred years, the Internet would be invented. It's all right there in black and white for all to read the sad story.

We made two or three trips back to the archives before we left Nova Scotia. I now had all the information I needed. Now I just had to write it in a book. I planned to name it *Don't Forget Maude: The Tale of Two Sisters.*

But before that happened, the book tour continued. Our next stop was Digby. The Scallop Festival invited us to take part. Not that we ate any scallops. Paul doesn't like them, and for me, they cost too much money. Since we were living off the book sales we made, I would have had to sell four books to eat scallops by myself.

Digby is famous for having the highest tides in the world. The wharfs built here were very tall, 50 feet or more. At low tide, the fishing boats were resting on dry land and accessed by very long ladders. They weren't going anywhere until the tide turned. At high tide you could jump in any boat from the wharf, no ladders needed. For three days, we watched the boats rise and then fall back down again. It was as if someone had taken the plug out of a bathtub.

We had dear friends who lived in Weymouth just outside Digby. We met them when we were first married and lived in Mill Village. Even though we moved away, we still have kept in touch all of these years. We were pleased to stay with Debbie and Bruce. It was so nice to be able to catch up on what has been happening in each of our lives. It certainly gave us a well-needed break from the camper. A real bedroom for a week.

It was also fun to make a presentation at Weymouth's library. Several of our friends and their families attended.

As you can read, our book tour was going very well, but I have to tell you that one time it didn't go as expected. After Digby, we were booked to go to a Bluegrass Festival in Kempt Shore. We arrived early and set up our camper in the designated place on the edge of a field. People started arriving shortly thereafter. They arrived toting instruments of every kind. There were fiddles, guitars, banjos, and big bass instruments being carried everywhere. They would just stop at someone's campsite, and a show would start. It was great music.

We felt a little out of place since we arrived with not an instrument in sight. All we had were books. Paul and I are not bluegrass fans, but anything live sounds pretty good. We enjoyed it. That is, we enjoyed it until midnight came and passed. At 3:00 a.m. we were trying to sleep. No one else was; they were still making music, and it was right beside our camper. Five a.m. it started to quiet down.

Paul said, "You had better sleep now. We have to get up in three hours."

Paul likes music. He even plays guitar that I gave him for Christmas several years ago. When we first met, we would make trips to Sheet Harbour to see my parents. He would allow me to drive his Chevrolet Biscayne, which was as big as a boat. I would drive and he would play the guitar. All the old country and western songs like 'He'll Have to

Go' and 'Four Walls' by Jim Reeves. I didn't even like country music.

However, even Paul said, "When you have heard "Folsom Prison Blues' for the fifteenth time and it is 3:00 in the morning, enough is enough."

We were selling books just to the right of the stage. They even had me come up on stage and advertise my book. However, we didn't have very many customers. We also heard they were going to jam all night again right outside our camper. I thought, *Great, I don't think I can take another night like last night. Paul even looked tired.*

"What are we going to do?" I asked.

"I think we should pack up and leave before everything gets started after dark."

That sounded good to me. We weren't selling books, and I was as tired as Paul. Paul went to talk to the guy who owned the farm. He told him it wasn't working out for us. We hadn't sold any books and planned to leave. Paul asked if there was any way to get money back.

It wasn't long before Paul returned. "Well, that didn't go very well. They aren't pleased that we're leaving. He even offered to move our campsite. If I'm going to pack up the camper, I'm certainly not going to unpack it again in the next field. So let's go pack up and go home."

"I guess you didn't get any money back?"

"No, not a cent."

That was the only place we lost money. We were thankful it wasn't very much.

It was almost the end of August. We were on our last leg of the tour. One of my favourite places to be in Nova Scotia is Cape Breton, a beautiful place, and it is also, where my brother Barry lives. He lives in a village called St. Peter's, one of the oldest settlements in North America. The open ocean is on one side of St Peter's and Lake Bras d'Or is on the other. It's as far east as you can go in North America. The other side of the ocean is England.

Barry and his wife, Gail, were great hosts to us the week we were there. Their house is right on Lake Bras d'Or. To sit and look out their window was a privilege indeed. It was like having a living picture on your wall. It continually changed from one minute to another. Boats would go by, clouds would change, and the sun would throw shadows in every direction. In the fall, the green would turn to orange, yellow, and red, and then the snow would come. A living picture worth more than gold.

Advertising was everywhere. Come to MacAskill Museum to hear an author speak about her book, *The Adventures of Captain Heman Kenney and Lady Catherine - 1833-1917*. She will be here for the weekend.

Back in February and March, when I was in my office in Covington, Indiana, I made reservations for this very book tour. I was speaking on the phone to Richard McMichaels, the head of The Maritime Museum of the Atlantic in Halifax, confirming the dates of the Tall Ships Festival. He knew I was setting up a tour. He suggested that I contact the MacAskill Museum. Well, I recognized the name immediately, for everyone who is from Nova Scotia knows of the famous photographer MacAskill. McMichaels even gave me a contact and a phone number. I asked him where the museum was. When he told me it was at St Peter's, Cape Breton, I couldn't believe it, for that is where my brother Barry lives.

I called Barry immediately and told him I was contacting the museum. He said, "Sister, if you get to come here, we will have a family reunion."

I made the call and spoke to Eva. She was thrilled and, before I knew it, I was booked for a weekend. Before I hung up, I told her I had a brother living in St. Peter's. If you live in St. Peter's, you know everyone, and everyone knows you.

She was surprised that she knew my brother Barry. Isn't it a small world?

Of course, I had to call Barry back. He couldn't believe I was actually coming. But here I was. I had been scheduled to make three presentations on August 14, 15, and 16 at the MacAskill Home Museum in St. Peter's.

Wallace MacAskill was a famous photographer in the early 1900s. He was known throughout the world, for he had won many awards for his pictures of schooners and marine scenes throughout Nova Scotia. My book about a schooner captain and his schooner the *Lady Catherine* fit right in.

I believe Barry was more nervous than I was about being there. Everywhere he went, he was asked if he was related to the author that was coming in with a book. Even when playing golf, a buddy of his asked about me. He had to say, "Yes, she is my sister."

Paul was helping me unload the things I needed for my first presentation from the car/truck. We walked along the walkway up to the stairs to the front door of the house, our arms loaded. This is the house where MacAskill lived as a boy. I managed to open the front door and, a moment later, I froze. Couldn't move another step.

"What's wrong? Paul asked. "Why have you stopped? This stuff is heavy you know. Why do you look like you've just seen a ghost?"

"Oh, no, Paul! Take a look over there on that cabinet."

It didn't take Paul long to see why I was so alarmed. "Why, it's the same picture you have on the front of your book."

"Oh, no, Paul, my publisher must have pirated that picture. I told him we couldn't use a picture of the *Bluenose* Schooner for my book. Canada owns the patent on anything about the *Bluenose*. MacAskill took many pictures of the *Bluenose*. That's why I thought it was the perfect picture for my book. It is the *Bluenose* and I didn't know it." Paul was the one who couldn't speak now.

"Here I am at the MacAskill Home Museum with a pirated picture of his on my book."

Eva, the director of the museum, was headed our direction. "Hello, Catherine, I just know it is you. Welcome to St. Peter's. I have been looking forward to your coming. You know I was talking to your brother Barry just yesterday."

"Yes, Barry mentioned he was talking to you." I was feeling sick to my stomach. "I think we have a problem that I didn't know anything about until just a few moments ago."

"Oh, can I be of help?"

I just handed her a copy of the book.

"It's a MacAskill; what a good looking book. This is marvelous; I am so glad you're here."

I was surprised by her reaction; she wasn't yelling yet. "But I didn't know it was a MacAskill picture until I saw. . ." I pointed to the cabinet. I believe my publisher may have pirated it and I had no idea."

"Don't worry at all. The patent is up and has been for years now. After fifty years anyone can use MacAskill's pictures."

"You have no idea how relieved I am. I can't believe I have a MacAskill picture on my book. A Nova Scotia story written in Indiana, and a famous Nova Scotia photographer's picture on the cover. Wait until I tell everyone."

The weekend was so much fun. I had an appointment to be interviewed on the local radio station, The Hawk, in Port Hawkesbury for a half hour. I was so nervous I couldn't eat breakfast the morning of the interview.

Paul had only one comment. "I have no doubt that you will do fine, my dear. I know you will have them eating out of your hand."

I laughed, "You always say that."

The interview lasted a half hour. After I got started, I wasn't nervous at all. We were given a copy of it. I handed it to Barry. I don't think he knew his sister had it in her. He was so happy for me that Gail and he gave me flowers.

We said our farewells to Barry and Gail. Barry might have a couple of things to think about after we leave. One would be that his sister Cathy could write better than he thought.

One more stop. It was August 31; our car/truck took us towards Antigonish and The Eastern Nova Scotia Exhibition. This was the beginning of the fall fairs in Nova Scotia.

Every town in Nova Scotia has a fall fair. The farmers bring their finest cattle, and their wives bring samples from their vegetable gardens and, of course, quilts, needlepoint, and other sewing projects. All of these things are judged, and everyone hopes for the red ribbons, but are satisfied to get a blue.

When we arrived, they showed us the place to put up our camper, right beside a fence in the parking lot. There was already a camper set up, much larger than ours was. However, that was nothing compared to the many huge rigs that came in later. They had living quarters, plus a place for horses to ride. We really looked funny, a popup camper jammed between several big rig trailers. We didn't mind; we were here to sell books.

We enjoyed seeing the horses perform in the arena, especially the Clydesdales. There were six of them pulling their shiny wagons. They reminded me of my mother. She was brought up on the prairie in Alberta, Canada. She could handle six horses. She had to take them through two gates to get to the field, where they were used to plow. My mother always had the strongest hands, even to this day at the age 89. I visited the barns and talked to those that owned the Clydesdales. They said my mother must have been a special lady. I told them they were right.

I met people that heard me on the Hawk radio program. They couldn't make it to the museum in St. Peter's but came here to buy a book. One thing about this whole tour was that we met so many nice people.

The nights were getting colder. We had to use a heater in the camper at night. Fall was certainly in the air.

"Well, are you ready?"

I saw the smile on Paul's face. "Ready for what?"

"I think it's time. Our trip of a lifetime is ending. Are you ready to head south?"

"It has been a trip of a lifetime, hasn't it? All things must end. Yes, I'm ready."

We headed back to Mill Village for our last weekend with them. Monday we went to Halifax to say goodbye to my mother. I have enjoyed being with her throughout this summer.

Before we could leave on Tuesday, September 9, a storm came ashore. The wind blew and the rain came down in torrents. It was a test for our little camper, but she kept us dry. We were ready to go, but couldn't put the camper down in the pouring rain. We waited and waited for the rain to stop. I prayed to God, "Just give us fifteen minutes, Lord, and we will have this camper down." It stopped raining.

"Quick, I yelled to Paul, let's get this thing down." Fifteen minutes later it started to pour rain again.

"You should have asked God for twenty minutes," Paul said. Paul and I had almost finished our task. However, we got it down, hitched to the car/truck, and headed down the highway on our way to Louisiana.

It didn't take us long to find out that it was harder traveling on the highways heading to Louisiana than it was being in Nova Scotia the whole three months. The days traveling were shorter than we liked. We had to stop no later than 6 p.m. Finding a campground and putting up the camper became a burden. It didn't help that Paul had injured himself and had a hernia. This meant that he could no longer lift anything heavy. It also meant he could not crank up the popup camper. So guess who had to do it. Me. Each time it took me a while; I had to rest three times before finally getting the camper up. I believe I developed muscles in my arms before arriving in Louisiana.

It took us an hour to put the camper up and an hour to take it down again. We never got back on the road in the morning until 10 a.m. The car/truck pulling our camper did not pass into Louisiana for ten days.

Our nightmare trip south included two flat tires on the camper. One time was in Tennessee; a very nice State Trooper came to our rescue and changed the tire for us. It wasn't easy since it was a very hot day.

To say the least, we were exhausted when we arrived in DeQuincy. We backed our camper into our own driveway. We had no desire to put it up and sleep there. We didn't have to. Our daughter, Jennifer, and friends had set up our bed mattress in our house on the floor of our bedroom. Nothing else was in the house. Not even electricity or water. We were lucky that the evening temperatures were cool enough that all we had to do was open our windows.

Our trip of a lifetime was over. We stayed eighty-one nights in the camper, a week at my brother Barry's house, a week at my sister Lois' house, and a week at our dear friends Debbie and Bruce's house. We were away for 102 days.

A funny thing is I, and I believe I can say, we, enjoyed the time we spent in that popup camper. Now that we were home and moved all of our furniture into our new house, we had no desire ever to sleep in the camper again. We sold it.

Maude is calling. I will put her story in this book.

Chapter Three

July 1893

121 Years Earlier

The stars in the night blackness were shining like diamonds on a piece of black velvet. The moon was full, and moonbeams shot out along the rim of the circle. The circle was as large as a fancy dinner plate -- the ones that were made of gold and very expensive. Angeline would never hold a gold plate, but her hand reached up to see if she could bring the moon down to her. *The moon belongs to everyone,* thought Angeline. She took the gold circle and put it in the pocket of her dress. She patted her pocket. *There. I will keep it safe. And whenever I need gold, I will reach into my pocket and there it will be.*

She smiled at herself. *How could I be so silly?* She knew how. She was on her way to see Vessell. She really shouldn't be on her way to see him. What would John Henry say if he knew? She left her oldest daughter, Sarah, to watch the brood. She was tired of the brood. Was she the only mother to think such a thing? She was tired of John Henry. Her gaze went towards the ocean. He was out there somewhere. The ocean saw him more than she did. He would come home, and before long, another baby would be there. *More work; all I do is work.*

However, not anymore. Not since she met Vessell Smith. He sort of came in with the wind. Put the wind in her sails that was missing for a long time. She didn't care about anything else. She just had to be with Vessell.

She stopped suddenly and looked at the moon. It was still there. *What would Vessell say? All I need is Vessell; he will take care of everything. I will go away with him. That's right; he will take me away from this island. He will take me to America. Sober Island will be history to me.*

A shiver went up her back. Darkness spread over her. She looked again, where the moon had been. Now it was gone. A dark cloud had overtaken it. A wind came in from the ocean, and she tightened her hold on her shawl.

Walking carefully, but earnestly, she focused on her journey. She was headed just on the other side of the forest-covered land. Her lantern now casts dark shadows along the way. Fear could be tasted in her mouth. She shook her shoulders. *Why should I be afraid? I've walked this way countless times.* It was low tide, and an eerie quiet filled her ears. The only sound was the light slapping of the salt water coming onto the beach.

Doubts climbed into her heart. *What have I done?* Her conscience kept asking that question. *I don't care,* Angeline silenced her conscience. *Vessell will know what to do. I know he will take care of everything.*

What about John Henry? Her conscience was there again. *Well, I should never have married him in the first place. I was so tired of the long hours in that cabin. Cooking, washing clothes, cooking, children crying, washing clothes. And when he did come home, he was dirty, tired and smelled like fish. He slept most of the time, and I was the one who was tired. Tired. Tired. Tired.*

What about the dance hall? Her conscience was speaking to her again. *The dance hall, you say. That was a lifetime ago.* Memories came to Angeline like the tide washing over her. She remembered the night John Henry came walking in. His hair was slicked back, his boots clean, and he had a sparkle in those brown eyes. *Oh, he couldn't dance, but he tried, and he laughed a great laugh when I taught him all I knew. We danced for hours just like a fairy tale. The music was playing just for us – a prince dancing with his princess.* The music turned to the sound of waves hitting the shore. She wrapped her shawl closer around her. Her mind told her, *that was a long time ago. Only a dream.*

The hoot of an owl brought Angeline back to the present. She walked faster; she was almost to the cemetery. Why they ever made the cemetery this close to the water was beyond her. There was always the same problem. At high tide, the water would enter the graves. You couldn't tell by looking, but once you dug a hole, you could see the water. Just thinking of it sent a shiver down Angeline's back.

She cleared her mind again. She could see the gravestones now. It was as if they were watching her. *Why are you here, Angeline? Why are you here?* Another shiver went down her back. There was a chill in the air, normal for Nova Scotia in July.

Just ahead, there was a huge, grey granite rock jutting out from the shore. It was just in front of the cemetery, and that was right where Angeline was headed.

It was deserted. *He isn't here yet?*

She crouched down, sitting on the hard rock. She drew her knees up and held them tightly. No one could see her. The sheet of granite rested just below the edge of the grass on the shoreline. It gave protection from the wind blowing off the water. Her eyes turned upward looking for the moon. All she saw were dark clouds. Closing her eyes tightly, the taste of fear was back in her mouth. *Everything will be all right.* She forced herself to say it repeatedly. *He will know what to do.*

The sound of footsteps on the rocks caused her to open her eyes. "Angeline, are you there?"

"Vessell, is that you?"

"Yes, Angeline, it's me." Sitting beside her, he took her hand into his. "It has been so long since I have seen you."

"Only four days, Vessell."

"Four days seem like an eternity." He took her into his arms. Now she felt safe. His lips searched for hers.

She backed away. "We must talk, Vessell."

"Now, what is there to talk about? We are together again; that is all that matters."

Fear in Angeline burst forward and tears fell from her eyes.

"What is it, Angeline? Has John Henry hurt you? Does he know?"

"No, John Henry doesn't know anything. I don't want him to know. Oh, Vessell, I'm pregnant."

Vessell pushed her away to look at her. "What?"

"I'm pregnant."

"I thought you took care of that. I thought you knew how. Who is the father?"

"You, of course."

"You have a husband, Angeline."

Angeline was shaking her head. "But you know John Henry is out fishing. He hasn't touched me in so long."

Vessell was on his feet. The small gravel was scattered as he walked up and down in front of Angeline.

"What are we going to do, Vessell?"

"What do you mean what are we going to do? You seem to be the one who has gotten yourself into this mess."

Angeline's fear was like bile in her mouth. She almost thought it was going to spill out on that very granite rock.

"I thought you loved me." Her eyes as bright as the stars that had been shining not long ago now stared at Vessell.

Vessell stopped pacing. "Of course, I love you."

"Then what are we going to do?"

Vessell started pacing again. "Angeline, I need to be back in Boston in one week. The lobster catch is being loaded on the ships in Sheet Harbour as we speak."

"Take me with you."

Vessell stopped again. "Do you know what you're saying?"

"Yes, Vessell, I want to go with you. I don't want to be without you. I want this baby to grow up with you, his father."

"But how?" Vessell couldn't picture this plan that Angeline was creating right in front of him.

"I could go on the boat with you. We could be together."

"Angeline, are you willing to leave everything behind?"

"Yes, to be with you."

Vessell paced back and forth on the rock. The silence was so quiet it hurt Angeline's ears. However, she would wait; Vessell was thinking. He would take care of everything. She just knew he would.

Vessell smiled. "This is what we will do. Angeline, you must be ready on Friday. The boat will leave on the high tide, which will be close to 8:00 in the morning. Meet me at the wharf at 7 a.m. I will make all the arrangements. Don't tell a soul. No one is to know until we're at sea and on the way to Boston. Bring everything you'll need in one bag. That is all, Angeline. One bag."

Vessell started to pace again. This time it was only in one direction. He was walking away straight down the beach. He was headed for Sheet Harbour.

Angeline drew her knees close together again. She held them tightly. *He didn't even kiss me goodbye,* she thought. She shook her head to clear her mind. *Well, he has a lot on his mind and a lot to do. I will see him on Friday. That is only three days away.*

Her hand went to her pocket. *If only I could take the gold from my pocket.* However, the moon was gone, and so was the gold.

Chapter Four

So Much for Love

Angeline was standing on the wharf in Sheet Harbour. She had watched the sunrise since she had been here two hours before. She had a dickens of a time getting here. Yesterday she had to make her children believe that she was deathly sick. She had her oldest running to her neighbour for help. The neighbour, the sweet old lady she was, was horrified to see the condition Angeline was in.

"Doctor," she said. "I need a doctor!"

The closest doctor was in Sheet Harbour and Angeline knew that. Just happened to be a boat going to Sheet Harbour that very afternoon. Therefore, Angeline packed her bag, headed away from Sober Island, and never looked back.

Arriving at the harbour just after suppertime, Angeline stood on the wharf hoping to find Vessell. There was more than one boat moored; she didn't know which one would be leaving for Boston in the morning. She found a fisherman's shack to rest in for the night. She left early since she wasn't sleeping well, and she was afraid the fishermen would arrive before sunup. She didn't want to meet any of them.

Here she was standing with her one bag waiting for 7:00 a.m. And, of course, Vessell. Her life was going to be changed forever in less than one hour. She watched as the gulls flew overhead. They were flying just for the thrill of it. Up in the blue sky, they waited for the first scraps of the day to be thrown their way. The wharf came to life slowly. Angeline watched men going about their work. Only one spoke to her. He wanted to know if he could help her in any way. She assured him she was fine and waiting for someone special.

Hunger pains visited her as well. How silly of her not to bring food. How long was it since she ate? Not since yesterday at breakfast. Maybe Vessell would have something for her. She began to look for him. She searched all the men's faces, but no one was familiar.

The same man who asked if he could help returned. "Are you still waiting for someone to meet you?"

"Yes." Angeline was beginning to worry.

"He must be running late."

"I don't know. Would you be so kind to tell me the time of day?"

"Of course." This man placed his hand in his pants pocket to retrieve an old gold watch. He placed his thumb on the lever, and the watch face was revealed. "It is twenty minutes after seven. Is he late?"

"Yes, he is." Angeline wondered what could be keeping him. "He told me to meet him right here at seven o'clock this morning."

"Maybe I could help. Who are you waiting for?"

"I'm to be on a boat going to Boston this morning."

Angeline could see the eyebrows on this man rise. "You must be mistaken. There's no boat leaving from here and going to Boston today."

"But there must be. This is Friday and the boat is to leave around 8:00 a.m. on the high tide, heading for Boston." Angeline just knew this man didn't know what was going on at the wharf. She started looking for Vessell. He must be here somewhere.

"You're right that the boat was to leave on high tide, but that boat left last night on the high tide. There's no other boat here to leave this morning. I suggest you go up to Conrod

House Hotel. Mrs. Conrod is a really nice lady, she is, and she will take good care of you." He was pointing his hand behind Angeline. "They keep records of all the boats that come and go from here. Maybe you got the wrong date."

Angeline was staring right through this man. She felt like she was just hit by a big rock. She could hardly move. "Yes, thank you. I will go up to the hotel and see what the problem may be." She turned herself around, holding onto her bag, and without looking back, she started to climb the hill.

Angeline felt like she was in some kind of cave. All the sound around her was echoing off the walls. However, there were no walls as she opened the door to enter the hotel. The Conrod House Hotel. She had passed by the hotel many times but never went inside.

In a trance, she walked up to the desk. Mrs. Conrod, the owner, was standing there going through papers. She looked up with a big smile. "Can I help you, deary?"

"I don't know. I thought I was to meet someone here this morning and then board a boat to Boston; however, there is no boat to Boston, and a man said it left last night on the high tide. And I don't know what to do."

"Well, let us see if we can straighten this out. There is no boat leaving today for Boston. Who were you to meet?"

"Vessell Smith."

"Vessell Smith?!" Mrs. Conrod was surprised to hear that name. "Why Vessell Smith spent an extended amount of time right here in this hotel. He checked out yesterday afternoon, and not too soon either. I'm afraid Vessell Smith left me holding the bag if you know what I mean. How do you know Mr. Smith?"

Angeline's mind was in turmoil. *Vessell Smith checked out yesterday. Vessell Smith left me holding the bag. How do I know Mr. Smith? How do I know anything? What does all this mean? No boat to Boston. I'm standing in Sheet Harbour waiting for Vessell -- and no Vessell.*

"How did you say you knew Mr. Smith?" Mrs. Conrod was waiting for an answer.

"He was just an acquaintance. I must have been confused with the date." Angeline's mind told her to just get out of there. She turned around, heading for the door. She wanted to run, just run. However, she managed to walk to the door, open it, and go through.

"Deary! Deary! Wait! Are you all right?"

Angeline didn't even hear her. Nor did she know Mrs. Conrod was already around the counter following her.

"Wait." Mrs. Conrod wasn't any spring chicken, but she could move quicker than one. She caught up with Angeline before she started down the hill to the wharf. "Wait." She took hold of Angeline's arm and turned her around. Angeline couldn't see anything, for her eyes were filled to the brim with tears. "Come with me." Mrs. Conrod led the way back to the hotel. Then Angeline allowed her to lead her. Her world had just collapsed, and she didn't care where she was going.

Mrs. Conrod opened the hotel door and led Angeline into to the sitting room. No one was there since it was still early in the morning. She sat Angeline down on the horsehair settee and helped her straighten her skirt. Mrs. Conrod had seen everything, being in the hotel business. She knew well what was happening here. Love spurned, that is how it looked to her. She took her favourite winged backed chair and placed it in front of the settee. After arranging herself in her chair, she reached out and took hold of Angeline's hands. "There, there now, deary, you can cry it all out." She patted her hands. "That Mr. Smith was just a no good scallywag. You're much better without him. Believe me, you're not the first to shed tears because of him."

But I loved him. Angeline's mind was screaming. *He loved me. We were going to have a life together. We. . .* The tears rolled down her cheeks again. *Scallywag. No, he wasn't. He was a fine man.* All these words were going through Angeline's mind. *It can't be. Vessell, where are you, why did you not come for me? Help me, Vessell. You were going to take care of everything.* Her heart was breaking as she sat on the settee.

"Now, now, deary. You are going to make yourself sick. Leslie is here and I will take care of you." Leslie reached into her pocket and took out a lace handkerchief. She began to fan it in front of Angeline's face. Finally, it looked like Angeline was coming back to the present. "That's better. You're going to be all right now. Leslie is here and will take care of you."

Angeline sat up straighter. "Leslie, who?"

"Leslie Conrod, you're in the sitting room of my hotel. Do you remember anything? What's your name?"

Angeline withdrew her hands from the old lady that was holding them. "I'm fine now. I must have felt faint there for a while."

"You do look pale. When did you eat last?"

Angeline searched her mind. *When did I eat last?* Her mind cleared. "Yesterday at breakfast."

Was it only yesterday that I was making breakfast for my children? Sarah, my oldest, was helping me. I ate pancakes. Then I made her believe I was ill. The tears started to flow again.

"Not again?" Leslie started waving the silk handkerchief. "You have to stop this. You have cried enough; he isn't worth it. Come into the kitchen. You'll feel better, and the world will look better too, as soon as you have had something to eat." Leslie pulled Angeline to her feet and led the way. Angeline was too weak to argue.

The kitchen had a big cook stove on one side. On the other was a work table, where two young girls were peeling potatoes and carrots. On the other side of the room was a small, round table. Here is where Angeline was sitting eating a roll with rhubarb. It was her third one, and she was starting to feel more like herself. Her life had changed in the last hour. She laughed, for it didn't change the way she thought it was going to.

"Glad to see you laugh." It was Leslie sitting down beside her. "You haven't told me your name or where you are from."

Angeline felt so embarrassed. *How can I tell this Leslie anything? My new life is starting now, sitting in Sheet Harbour in the Conrod Hotel's kitchen, talking to an old lady named Leslie. Didn't make it very far from Sober Island, did I? What in the world, am I going to do now?* Tears would have started flowing again, but she didn't allow them. She was mad now. *How could Vessell do this to me? That no good . . . What did she call him? A scallywag?*

"You aren't going to tell me your name?" Leslie was starting to worry about this lady.

"Angeline. My name is Angeline."

"Well, that's a beginning. So Vessell said he would meet you here this morning?"

Angeline's wounded eyes looked up at her. I thought he loved me. I guess I was wrong, wasn't I?" The truth was starting to sink in for Angeline.

"Angeline is a very pretty name. I'm sorry to say that he didn't love you. If he had, he wouldn't have run out on you. You're better without him. Believe me."

Angeline could not believe anything. All she knew was that her heart was broken.

"Where are you from, Angeline?"

Angeline let out a sigh. *I have to tell her sometime.* "Sober Island."

"How did you get here from Sober Island?" Leslie was surprised. You could only get to Sober Island by boat.

"I came in by boat last evening."

"My goodness, where did you spend the night? Never mind, maybe I don't want to know."

"I spent the night in a fisherman's shack. I'm not what you think."

"No, of course not, you don't even look like that. How are you going to get back?"

"I don't know; I wasn't planning to go back."

"Do you have any money?"

"Vessell . . ."

"I know, Vessell was going to take care of that too. Wonderful, Vessell is still costing me money."

"Then I must leave." Angeline didn't want to be owing to anyone.

"Sit back down, Angeline. I said I would help you and I meant it. We women have to help one another, so don't you worry none. Leslie will figure out something. Have another roll and I will be back in a few moments."

Angeline was alone. Even the two young girls had left the kitchen to continue their work. Alone. She would be alone now for the rest of her life. What would John Henry say and do when he found out the truth? A shiver went down her back. She would have to face the music when it happened. She wouldn't think of it now. Tears were spilling from her eyes again. It didn't matter; no one was there to see.

*****

Angeline was standing on a wharf holding tightly to her bag. Another wharf, not Sheet Harbour's main wharf. Not where she was waiting for the boat to take her away with Vessell to Boston. Those plans had crashed and burned. This was a smaller wharf. This was the East River.

Leslie had found her a ride on a wagon. A peddler was going to East River. Leslie also talked to a guest staying at the hotel. He had a schooner leaving that day heading towards Halifax. He accepted a free night stay in the hotel on his next run to Sheet Harbour. All he had to do was drop off a lady to Sober Island. It wasn't even out of his way.

Angeline was standing on the East River Wharf. She could see the schooner in front of her. Her name was written on the bow: *Sarah Lee*. Pain struck her heart again. Not for Vessell, but for her first-born, Sarah. How could she have done all this to her family? She sure made a mess of her life. Now she had to live with it. But, how?

Up East River, she could see the ferry coming towards the landing. The ferry had a horse and wagon onboard. The men were pulling the ropes with all their strength. Each pull brought them closer to the landing. The wagon looked to be filled with fish. The man on the wagon was a fish peddler coming from Watt Section Wharf. The fishermen must have come in with a good catch that day.

Her attention was drawn back towards the wharf and the schooner *Sarah Lee*. A man was walking towards her. "You coming aboard? We want to get underway before the tide turns." Without a word, she followed him. He found a bench for her to sit on. "I'm afraid this is all I have for you to sit on. I don't take passengers very often."

"That will be fine, thank you." Angeline wasn't very thankful. She was on her way back to Sober Island. She felt sick to her stomach. It wasn't the food she had received from Leslie. Without Leslie, she didn't know what she would have done. And it wasn't because of the baby she was carrying. No, she hadn't forgotten the baby. Her stomach was sick because she was going back to her old life. The life she hated.

Chapter Five

The Innocence of a Baby

The Cook Settlement on East River, Sheet Harbour was a thriving community. Thanks to the lumber mill, the government wharf, and Lowe's Ferry, there was lots of activity.

The lumber mill employed 35 men. It kept busy, for the pulp boats guided the trees cut by the lumberjacks straight to the wharf at East River.

Lowe's Ferry was on the other side of the river. Traffic along the main road coming from Port Dufferin and Watt Section kept Elbridge Lowe busy. Many times, he was awakened at night from his sleep. A night traveler needed to cross over to Sheet Harbour. Elbridge tried to tell everyone he was closed from 10:00 p.m. to 6:00 a.m., but there would be people banging on his door at all hours of the night. His wife, Agnes, was always afraid the banging would wake the baby. Elbridge would reluctantly pull on his pants and boots and stumble to the ferry, but he charged them a nickel more just for getting him out of bed.

Come 6:00 a.m. he would be busy all day. He would charge fifteen cents for two horses and a wagon, and five cents a person. Everyone knew the routine. The ferry could hold two wagons, or a wagon and buggy, and no more than four horses. Everyone onboard would have to help pull the ropes. Depending on how heavy the load, it would take 15 minutes to cross to the other side of the East River to the landing where Mr. Hall's house stood. Of course, in winter, when the ropes were cold and slippery, and you had to deal with ice flows, it would take much longer. At the landing, and right past Mr. Hall's house, there was a fork in the road. One way headed towards the government wharf, the other straight to Sheet Harbour. Just past there, the road that turned to the right was called East River Road. There is where you would find Cook Settlement. Just as the name indicated, many Cook families lived there. The road that went to the left was called Cook Road. It went straight up the hill into the woods. East River Road continued along the East River bank until you came to the lumber mill.

Ed lived his whole life here. His parents lived halfway up Cook Road in the house his grandfather had built. Ed had six brothers -- himself in the middle. His father deeded land to them all. Ed chose twenty-five acres at the very top of the hill. As a young boy, he would climb the hill, clearing a pathway through the woods until he reached the very top. There he would sit and look down. He could see the blue ocean. Well, not really the ocean. It was Sheet Harbour Passage -- salt water for sure. The schooners would be coming through the passage, heading towards the many wharfs along Sheet Harbour.

More than once, he got into trouble with his father. He couldn't be found when his father needed him. Ed watched the schooners come and go from his view just over the trees and just under the clouds.

Ed grew up and married Flora McQuarrie. He met her one summer when she was visiting Sheet Harbour from Cape Breton. They were married in 1879. They lived with his older brother, Alfred, and his wife, Mary, and their five children, four of whom were girls. Flo fit right in with the family. Ed and Flo spent every spare moment building a house on the top of the hill.

That was nine years ago. Today Ed and Flo were raising two little girls. Maude and Catherine, known as Kate, were the loves of Ed's life. There had been two other babies at the beginning of their marriage: two boys -- both still born. Ed thought Flo would die of a broken heart, but time heals, and two little girls helped mend both their hearts.

March came in like a lion and stayed that way. Winter did not want to leave. Ed was thinking spring might have passed them by this year. He pulled the collar of his wool coat up to protect his neck from the cold wind. He had a wool muffler around his neck. Flo made it for him this past Christmas.

It wasn't snowing yet, but he could see the clouds turning darker and darker. They were getting closer to the ground. Ed wished he could reach up and push them away. Sheet Harbour didn't need another snowstorm; however, whether they needed it or not, a snowstorm was coming.

He had just left the warmth of his house. Flo gave him porridge with brown sugar and warm milk. In fact, he had eaten two bowls. The girls were still asleep, since it was still early, just before daybreak. Flo would have time just for herself until they filled her day with activity.

Ed started his way down the hill. He smiled to himself. He thought of using a sled to get himself to the bottom, but he knew Maude and Kate would surely miss it. He smiled because he even thought about using a sled, not because his daughters would miss it. Ed looked down at his military boots. Last fall a peddler came by. A curious sight, he had several pairs of boots and was carrying them around his neck. Ed stopped him right on the spot and found the pair that fit his feet the best. With two pairs of Flo's knitted wool socks, his feet had been warm all winter. The boots didn't allow him to slip and slide. This was good for coming back up the hill, but going down -- he still wished he could slide.

Ed was headed to the shipbuilding yard at East River. Thankfully, he had worked there all winter. Soon the schooner would be christened the *Highland Mary*. He was proud to be a part of building her, for she was a fine schooner.

Both Daniel Wright and John Farnell, the owners of the shipyard, were there when Ed arrived. This was a special day indeed, for he had only seen his bosses twice before. They called the workers together and thanked Ed and his co-workers for a good job they had done. He and the other workers were in a jolly mood as they worked on the final stages of the schooner.

A young man came into the shipyard. Ed looked up and saw it was Jack. Ed knew Jack well. Jack, who worked on the government wharf, helped unload all the schooners that came to the wharf. However, today he was looking for Ed. "Ed, I have a message for you."

"Who from?" He was placing his hammer down. Jack handed him a piece of paper. Ed opened it and began to read.

Dear Ed,

Please come.

Your brother,

John Henry

"Who was this message from?"

"Captain Albert Jones was told to get the message to you. The *Foaming Billow* has just come in at the wharf from Sober Island."

The workers gathered around Ed. "Is it bad news?"

"I don't know. It's from my brother. He just said, "Come.""

"That be John Henry?"

"That's right. I haven't seen him since last spring."

After speaking with Mr. Wright and Mr. Farnell, Ed was now at the wharf looking for Captain Albert Jones. Ed was told the captain was making a trip back to Sober Island the next day. That is if the storm blew itself out to sea. Ed paid the one-dollar fare for the trip.

*****

"If John Henry needs me, I must go." Ed was talking it over with Flora. "The storm will be over by morning."

"Stopped snowing now." Maude was looking out the window.

"I will pack you a bag." Flo went into the bedroom.

"Plus, a lunch would be great too." Flo heard his request.

"How long will you be gone?" Kate was sitting close to her father.

"I don't know, little one. I will be back as soon as I can. You can look out at the ocean and watch for me to return."

"Oh, Papa, Papa, how will I know which boat will be you?"

"Well, it won't be a big schooner and it won't be a row boat."

"It's a coaster." Maude finished the sentence for her father.

"What's a coaster?"

"It's a small boat that goes along the coast of all the small communities in Nova Scotia." Maude was pleased she knew the answer.

"That's right, Maude.

*****

Ed arrived on Sober Island late afternoon on the next day. The snowstorm had passed, making it clear and cold. The blue sky and the blue water were even bluer than any bucket of blue paint. Oh, but it was cold, and the wind blew the waves up on the bow of the boat. Ed spent most of the trip sitting on a circle of ropes that were placed in a corner below deck. This gave him time to eat the lunch Flo had made and wonder what his brother needed.

Ed was familiar with Sober Island. He knew where his brother lived and headed up the road. He stopped, for he was troubled by what he saw ahead. On the front door of the house hung a black wreath, and people were going in and out.

Who has died? He was in a hurry to find John Henry. Without removing his coat, he searched through those gathering at the house. "Where is John Henry?" He was directed to the drawing room.

Ed found John Henry sitting on a bench close to a freshly built pine coffin. "John Henry," Ed spoke softly.

John Henry raised his head to see Ed. "Ed, you have come. I knew you would."

"What has happened?" Ed was afraid to look in the coffin.

"Angeline, Ed. It's Angeline, she is gone."

"Where are the children?" Ed didn't know why he asked. He looked around the drawing room.

"Sarah is taking care of it."

Just then, Sarah came into the room. Following her were her siblings. And in her arms, she was carrying a baby -- a very young baby.

Ed allowed himself to look in the coffin. Angeline was lying there with her hands folded. Then he looked over to the young baby Sarah was holding. "I didn't know you were expecting another baby."

"I didn't either. Sarah, please take that out of here."

Sarah obeyed her father, and she and the other children departed to wherever they had come from.

"Did Angeline die in childbirth?" Ed noticed his brother didn't want anything to do with the baby.

"No, I wish she had!"

"Then, John Henry, you're going to have to explain."

"The children don't know." John Henry looked to see if the children had left the room. "The baby is not mine. The baby" – he looked at Angeline lying in the coffin – "is not ours."

Ed sat down on the bench with a thud beside his brother. "What happened to Angeline?"

"She left the house four nights ago. Allen MacClaud found her body on the beach the next day. Fine thing she went and done, Ed. Fine thing." John Henry was shaking his head.

*****

There were but a dozen people at the cemetery. Angeline once again returned to the cemetery where she had put the moonbeams in her pocket. This time she couldn't see the moon. This time there was no dreaming about the future. Her eyes were shut, and her dreaming had ended.

Reverend Meadu did the best he could under the circumstances. "Ashes to ashes. Dust to dust. May Angeline's soul rest in peace."

Sarah and the other little ones seemed to look straight past the mound of earth that remained. John Henry turned and walked back to the waiting wagon. He was still shaking his head. The children followed him since they didn't know what else to do. Ed untied the horses and climbed into the wagon, and they headed back home.

After everyone had gone home, Ed was sitting by himself looking out the window. The white caps on the water were churning back and forth. Sarah came into the room. She was by herself, except for holding the baby in her arms. "Uncle Ed."

"Yes, Sarah." Ed didn't know what to say to the child. Sarah was sixteen, but looked much older.

She held the baby out to him. "You had better take him. Father doesn't want him around. I can take care of the others, for I have always done so. But this baby will do better if he is raised someplace else."

Ed sat holding the baby. "A boy -- and John Henry doesn't want him." He watched the baby sleep.

Chapter Six

Don't Mess With Me!

urse this mud. Ed was walking up Cook Road. Mud was ankle deep and it was everywhere. Spring had finally shown herself. The warmer temperatures melted the snow, and there was a lot to melt that year. Once the snow was gone, the red-brown mud appeared. And slippery -- it was much slicker than the snow and ice that had melted. It was the kind of mud Flo liked. He smiled to himself, knowing she really didn't like it. She had the dickens of a time washing it out of his and the children's clothes. However, Flo would get buckets full of the slimy, red-brown mud, add straw or even sawdust, and then turn it into bowls and plates, which would be left out in the sun until fall. Those that survived, she would call her new dishes.

Ed cleared his mind to the present. He had to be very careful where he placed his feet. He didn't want to fall -- not because it would wound his pride or get him wet and dirty. It was because he was carrying a precious package. A baby boy. Ed looked down to see the eyes peeking out through a homemade quilt that was wrapped around him. Ed sure had many men staring at him on his journey home. Thanks to Sarah, he had everything he needed in a canvas bag, which was slung over his shoulder. He had enough milk for one more feeding. Goat's milk placed in a glass quart milk bottle, the kind a milkman leaves at your door. That is if you don't have a cow.

Ed was concentrating too hard on his walking to think of what he had left behind in Sober Island. There had been plenty of time to think of that on his return to Sheet Harbour. *What will Flo think?* Ed looked at the boy. "Well, I guess we will find out in just a few moments, won't we?

The sun was setting just over the trees when Ed turned into the pathway to his home. He could see the girls had spread the ashes from the cook stove along the walking path. The mud wasn't quite as slippery. No one was outside, so he headed for the back door. Opening the door, his eyes looked around to the familiar sight. He was home. The scene that played out filled him with peace and love.

Flo turned around from the cook stove. "Ed, it's you! Thank God you made it home safely." She was halfway across the kitchen. "Girls, your papa is home!"

They already knew, for Kate and Maude had left the table, where they were busy doing schoolwork.

"Papa, you're here." Everyone was rushing towards Ed.

Ed put his hand up. "Whoa!" It was as if he was slowing down horses with the reins. "Slow down, be careful." He was still holding onto his precious package.

Flo stopped just before her husband. "Edward Cook." She only used his full name on rare occasions. "What do you have there?"

"Papa, did you bring a gift from Sober Island?" Kate was jumping up and down clapping her hands.

"You all must be very quiet." He was speaking to Kate. "Yes, I did bring a gift from Sober Island."

"Bring it over to the table." Flo was moving lesson books to make room.

Ed put the wrapped quilt on the table. Slowly and very carefully, he began to open it. There lay the baby in a white flannel gown, a green knitted sweater, and matching bonnet. Ed was amazed that the baby was still sleeping.

"A baby." Maude was the first to speak.

Kate was climbing onto a chair to get a better look. "Is it a baby doll?"

"No, silly, it's a real baby." Maude knew a real baby when she saw one.

Ed looked up at Flo. She was staring at the baby, knuckles between her teeth. She looked back at Ed. Ed was smiling.

"For pity's sake, Ed, where did you get this baby?"

"It's a long story, for your ears only. Let's just say I brought him home to live with us."

"Him. . ."

"Yes, a boy, Flo. It's funny how God works sometimes. We have our boy."

The baby began to stretch his little arms above his head. He opened his dark eyes, looking around him.

"He's looking at me." Kate liked this gift from Sober Island.

"But, Ed, I have nothing. How can we take care of a baby?"

"Don't worry." Ed reached for the canvas bag. Thanks to Sarah, we have everything we need. Well, at least for the night." Ed looked down at the bottle of milk. "Well, maybe not. You feed him this." He handed the bottle to Flo. "Mom and Dad have a goat. I'll go get some milk." He was out the door as he spoke.

Ed was back in less than an hour. His journey would have been quicker if the goat had cooperated. Nanny goat was not accustomed to being milked so late in the day. In addition, Thomas and Deborah Cook, his parents, didn't know what to think of the story about a new baby at Ed's house. He left with the promise he would return the next day and explain everything. On the way back to the house, Ed stopped at his shed. He remembered a wooden box there. It would make a good bed, at least until he could get the baby cradle down from the attic. He brought it with him.

Ed opened the back door. This time the scene was completely changed. His girls hardly noticed he had entered. Flo was rocking the baby in the rocking chair by the cook stove. The same rocking chair she rocked Maude and Kate in when they were babies. On either side of her were the girls watching their mother holding the newest member of their family.

As Ed and Flo lay in the darkness before going to sleep, Flo had tears in her eyes, for it was hard for her to hear such a sad story. "Ed, I am glad you brought this baby home. Just like you said, God works in mysterious ways, and we now have a son. Does he have a name?"

"No, he doesn't. I have been thinking about it on the way back from Sober Island. I would like to name him after me, for he will be Edward Cook Jr.

"That sounds good. Edward Cook Jr., it will be."

*****

"Kate, it's your turn to run after Edward." Maude was tired out. "Quick, Kate, he's running towards the chickens -- and he has a stick."

Kate jumped off the back step. "Why doesn't he like those chickens?"

"I wish I knew. I have never seen a three-year-old attack chickens. Edward likes to see the chickens fall over after he hits them."

"No, Edward. Give me that stick." Edward wasn't listening to Kate. He was running around the chickens, swinging the stick as he went. "Papa is going to get you." Edward stopped in his tracks. "So you remember yesterday, do you?"

"Papa is bad."

"No, Papa is not bad. You are, Edward. You cannot hit the chickens with a stick."

"Papa hit me with a stick."

"Yes, and did you like it?"

"No!" Edward was sure of that.

"The chickens don't like it when you hit them with a stick." Kate took Edward's hand and led him back to the house. "Mother may be baking cookies. Let's go and see."

Edward allowed Kate to lead him away.

*****

Flo walked up the steps of East River School. There was a time she was happy to come here. Both Maude and Kate always did well here. This would be the last year for Maude. Where did the time go? Maude was almost grown up. A fine strong woman she would be. Kate turned out to be a beauty. Flo worried the beauty would go to her head. Flo also knew Kate was Ed's favourite, even though he made sure Maude didn't know. However, Flo knew. Kate was the beauty, but Maude had more common sense.

Flo wasn't at the school for Maude or Kate. She was there because of Edward. Mrs. Miller, Edward's teacher, was at her wit's end. A week didn't go by without Edward fighting with the other boys. He also picked on the girls. Flo and Ed tried their best at home. More than Flo could count, they punished the boy. Ed took the switch to him, but to no avail. It was as though Edward enjoyed getting into trouble.

It was the smile on the boy's face that disturbed Flo the most.

Somehow, the story that his real mother took her life had spread throughout East River and Sheet Harbour, and no telling how far. Ed and Flo never spoke of it. Not since the day, Ed brought the baby to live with them. Surely, Edward knew he was loved. After all, he was named Edward Junior. How the story got out was beyond them; they knew it hurt Edward and the girls as well. Every day they had to listen to the taunts of the older boys at school. The girls talked in whispers one to another. Edward said he would fight them all -- and he did.

Maude had no patience with Edward. He was to blame for every problem she had at school. She was known as the big sister to *that boy*.

Kate, on the other hand, loved Edward dearly. She stood up for her brother. Kate was always able to calm Edward down when he was angry. Edward felt Kate was his only friend. He would do anything for her.

Edward hated school because kids made fun of him. He mainly went because Ed and Flo expected him to go. In addition, of course, he went because of Kate; however, he looked forward to the day he would quit. Edward wasn't close to Ed, the only father he ever knew. He was never told who his real father was. The only one who knew was his mother, Angeline, and she took it to her grave. There were two reasons why Edward wasn't close to Ed: one was he wasn't his real father; the other was Ed was always working, for times were hard, and Ed worked wherever he could find a job.

The first time Edward heard the story about his mother killing herself, he didn't believe it. It was the day Doug, a bigger boy, had him cornered on the schoolyard. In a second, Doug had Edward pinned to the ground, mashing dirt into his face. "Your mother was no good, and she killed herself all because of you," he yelled.

In tears, Edward went home. That same night he had a long talk with his father. Tears running down his face, he told Ed what was said. He looked into his father's eyes telling him he didn't believe what Doug had said. Why would Doug say things like that?

Ed had known this day would come. He thought he was prepared, but he wasn't. He looked into his son's eyes and told him that everything Doug said was true. Ed saw his son's heartbreak that day. Edward had never been the same. Anger had set in and it never left.

Ed didn't tell his son the whole story. Ed didn't know the whole story and had never asked his brother John Henry about it. It didn't matter, and he wanted Edward to feel the same way. It did not matter. Ed loved Edward Jr. as his own son, and that was that. Edward could not feel the same way.

The boys that taunted him seemed to know more about his life than he did. The more they said the worse Edward beat them. There came a point when no one would say a word to Edward, for now, everyone feared him.

That's just what Edward wanted -- to be feared. No one would mess with him.

Chapter Seven

I Call Her Kate

own at the village of Watt Section, Alexander Kenney was preparing to light the gas lantern at the lighthouse. Alexander knew just how to do it, for he had been doing it since a child. His father, Heman, had taught him, and when he was away on trade trips on his schooner *Lady Catherine,* Wayne continued the lessons. Every evening Wayne and Alexander had walked across the field towards the lighthouse. They carried hot coals from the wood stove in the kitchen to light the oil lamp. When lit, the light was so large that Heman remembered thinking it was as big as the sun.

Wayne was a good teacher. To this day Wayne was more like an uncle to Alexander than just a labourer hired by his father. Wayne was family. He had quite a colourful history. He came to the Show House just after it was built, looking for work. His last hope of finding a job was here with the Kenney family. Wayne had been to the wharf and begged the fishermen to teach him to fish, but to no avail. He went to the shipbuilding yard and even thought about being a lumberjack, but no one would hire him. Wayne had a big problem, not that he thought it was a problem; he was used to having only one arm.

Alexander remembered well how his father told the story. Wayne was a thin, scrawny young man with dark circles under his eyes when he showed up at the Kenney's place. He was a desperate man. Heman never forgot what Wayne said.

"Before you say no, or you are not interested, let me tell you something. I can and will work harder than any two or three men that you have ever known. My right arm is strong and can do anything a man with two arms can do. You won't be sorry if you hire me."

That was 30 years ago. No one in the whole family was sorry Heman hired Wayne, for they loved him. Many things had changed since then at the Kenney place. The great Show House burned down when he was just a child. Heman, his father, was resting peacefully up on the hill overlooking the ocean in St Andrew's Cemetery. His five sisters were married and gone, raising families of their own.

Elizabeth, Alexander's mother, lived with him in the little blue cottage that had taken the place of the Show House.

"What are you doing, son?" The voice of Elizabeth brought Alexander back from the past. "Looked like you were somewhere far away." Elizabeth smiled at him.

"That I was. I was thinking of the time when Wayne first came. It was way before I was even born. But I remember Father telling the story."

"It seems like Wayne has always been a part of this family. He helped raise every one of you." Elizabeth slowly sat down in the rocking chair beside the cook stove. "How is he?"

"Wayne? Oh, Wayne is fine. He's in his room in the barn. I checked on him no more than an hour ago. He wanted to tend to the light this evening. I managed to get him to let me do it."

"It's not time yet, is it?" Elizabeth looked up at the cuckoo clock, "Not even 6 o'clock; the days are getting longer now that it is March."

"Well, that's what I was about to tell you. I'm going out tonight. There is a dance in Sheet Harbour at the United

Church hall. Therefore, I'll be lighting the lamp early for the lighthouse. Do you need anything, Mother? I can do it right after going to the lighthouse."

"No, son, you go on." Elizabeth had noticed a change in Alexander. There was a spring in his steps; his mind seemed to be in the clouds, and a smile would appear on his face. "Are you meeting anyone special?" She smiled as she asked the question.

Alexander looked towards his mother. "Can't keep anything from you, can I? As a matter of fact, yes, I'm meeting someone special."

"What is her name?"

"Catherine Cook; I call her Kate."

"Is she pretty?"

"Very pretty indeed. All of our friends want her to enter the beauty pageant being held at the school. I told her she would win."

"Does she live in Cook Settlement?"

"Yes, half way up to Cook Road. She has an older sister, Maude, and a younger brother, Edward. Ed and Flora are her parents. She is known as Flo. Mother, do you know them?"

"I'm not sure. I may have heard our dear neighbour, Maude Rood, speak of them."

"Mother, may I bring her? I would like you to meet her."

"You know, Alexander, your father had a Catherine he loved dearly."

Alexander laughed. "Yes, he had his *Lady Catherine,* didn't he? The best schooner in all the Eastern Shore. That's what they used to say. I miss the *Lady Catherine,* don't you Mother?"

"Yes, dear, I miss her. But, don't worry. I still see her once in a while."

Alexander raised his eyebrow. "I know, Mother. Just on the other side of the lighthouse, coming out of the mist."

"That's right," she smiled at her son. "Now you had better go to the lighthouse. We wouldn't want you to keep Catherine waiting, would we?"

"No, Mother. I call her Kate."

*****

Kate did win the beauty contest. Alexander won her heart, and a wedding was planned for the end of March. Elizabeth was making Alexander a wedding suit. She used the dining room table and had the fabric and pattern scattered throughout the room. It was times as these she missed her sewing room the most. Heman had made her a lovely sewing room on the second floor of the Show House. However, those days were long gone. Time was spoken of before the fire and after the fire. The sewing room was before the fire. Elizabeth would make do sewing on the dining room table. She was happy knowing, thanks to her father; she knew how to make a fine man's suit. Before she was married, she worked with her father, James Finlay, at his textile factory in Halifax. The textile factory was well known for making men's suits. She had fond memories of that time, for that was where she met Captain Heman Godfrey Kenney, the love of her life.

Alexander and Kate's wedding was to take place at the United Church in Sheet Harbour, where the Cooks were members. There was to be a reception in the church hall.

Elizabeth, Alexander and his sister, Mary Elizabeth, husband Eric Rood, Eric's parents, Maude and Dan Rood, and all the little Roods traveled together. Wayne was aboard the wagon, since he wasn't going to be left behind. It made a tight fit, but most everyone was sitting on the wood planks that were used for seats.

The morning of March 30, they awoke to heavy frost, and a light layer of ice covered the puddles that formed the day before from the last of the melting snow. The sun was shining, and the lighthouse seemed to be shimmering in the early morning light. The ocean looked so blue; maybe those fishermen painted it as they passed the lighthouse, heading out for another day to fill their nets with fish.

Everyone was bundled up, as if it was the middle of winter. Molly and Rosie, the horses, pranced and snorted steam from their nostrils, as the Rood's wagon rounded the well, heading out of the Kenney's laneway. These two horses were almost part of the Rood's family, for they had owned them for so long. Dan Rood trusted them with his life. He and Eric sat up front. Dan held back on the reins tightly, for Molly and Rosie really wanted to run. They turned right as they left the laneway passing in front of his home. He guided the horses left again and up the hill towards the cemetery. Elizabeth couldn't help looking left at the cemetery gate. Her gaze went to where Heman's grave was placed.

"Don't worry about, Alexander, my dear. He's doing just fine," she whispered.

"Did you say something, Mother?" Mary Elizabeth asked. "There's so much noise I could not hear you."

"Just saying it's a wonderful day for a wedding, my dear. A wonderful day."

A half hour later, they came upon Lowe's Ferry. Elbridge saw them coming and began preparing the ferry for the crossing of the East River. Molly and Rosie didn't seem to mind being led onto the ferry. They had done this before, and it was familiar to them.

Eric paid the 35-cent fare and they were on their way. Eric, Alexander, Dan, and Wayne did their share, helping Elbridge pull on the thick mighty rope that edged them closer to the other side of the river.

The wind was cold in the middle of the river. Mary Elizabeth bundled up the little ones. Elizabeth wrapped her scarf right around her neck. She was thinking she was ready for spring. *I hoped April would be warmer.*

Elbridge slapped Alexander on the back. "Congratulations! May you and your new wife be happy from this day and all the many days of your life."

"Thank you," Alexander replied as he climbed back on the wagon.

"Farewell!" They all waved as the horses took them onto the road. It did not take long before they could see the church on the right. Elizabeth noticed that several other wagons were already there.

It was crowded in the coatroom, as they discarded coats and unbundled everyone. Looking into the sanctuary, satin white bows had been placed on the end of each pew. Upon the altar were large candles. No flowers could be seen.

March was too early for flowers. The left side of the church was almost full. The Kenney family from far and near had arrived early. Elizabeth was surprised to see Moses and John Charles all the way from Halifax. Moses and John Charles were crewmates of the *Lady Catherine.* They worked alongside Heman right up to the day he died.

Moses and John Charles stepped towards Elizabeth, taking turns giving warm hugs. "We have come to see Alexander married off. Heman would have wanted us present and accounted for," added John Charles.

Moses looked down at his clothes. "Seems like we should be wearing the green and beige dress colours of the *Lady Catherine."*

"Moses, you always looked so handsome in the dress uniform of the *Lady Catherine."* Elizabeth was experiencing a flashback. She could see Moses; his hair slicked back wearing a green vest, a green jacket, and canvas-coloured trousers. At his neck was cloth that matched the ribbon on the green vest. Embroidered on the ribbon were the words, *Lady Catherine.* Then, of course, a canvas-coloured cap. The vision parted and she could see Moses clearly. "But that's alright, Moses, that was before the fire."

"Yes, that was before the fire," Moses repeated.

Alexander stepped in. "Welcome to you both. You should have stayed with us. You know you are always welcome."

"Let me shake your hand. Just look at him, John Charles. A spitting image of his father. Captain Kenney would be so proud – may he rest in peace." Then Moses took his hand towards his chest and crossed himself.

Many more people entered the church, and it was not long before the right side of the church began filling up. The bride, Kate, had lots of family and friends who were present to see the happy couple exchange wedding vows.

The ceremony was a happy one. Elizabeth even managed not to cry. After all, this was her baby, the last of them to leave the nest. She didn't have to use the white embroidered hanky she placed inside her long white gloves.

The receiving line gathered at the front of the church, for it was far too cold to have it near the doorway. Elizabeth met many of Kate's family. She showed interest when Alexander presented Kate's sister and her husband, Maude and John Winslow Kenney to her. "Are we related to all the Kenney families in the area?"

Elizabeth couldn't help making the obvious statement. "Maude, your sister is marrying into the Kenney family also. Your names will be the same."

"Yes, isn't that amazing? Little sister is really following in my footsteps."

"John," Elizabeth turned towards Maude's husband. "I know there are many Kenney families in this area. I'm not sure if we're related."

"Yes, your husband, Heman, and I had the same grandfather, Isaac Kenney. He married twice. I was from the second marriage. I believe that makes us some kind of cousins."

Alexander broke the spell. "Mother, there's a backup in the line." He motioned to those in the line behind Elizabeth, who were patiently waiting to give their best wishes to the newly married couple.

"Oh, of course, pardon me," Elizabeth greeted the lady next to Maude. However, all she could think of was that Heman and John Winslow were cousins. *How interesting,* she thought. She would look more into that later.

Everyone had passed through the line and made their way to the church hall for the reception. Only the bridal party remained. Elizabeth took hold of Kate's hand. Placing it into Alexander's hand, she spoke, "From this day forward you will be my daughter. Alexander loves you and I will love you." She looked into her son's eyes. "I love you both."

The wedding dinner was delightful, thanks to the Cook family. When no one could eat any more of the delicious food, the young people pushed the tables and chairs up against the walls. Now there was room to dance. The men appeared towards the front bringing stools to sit on. They also brought a fiddle, guitar, and bass fiddle, and they tapped their feet as the music began.

Kate and her father, Ed, took to the dance floor. Everyone clapped as they danced around the room. Ed motioned for Alexander to join them. Ed gave up his daughter to Alexander. Alexander took Kate into his arms and glided her around the room. Everyone clapped. Then, as if by magic, everyone was dancing.

Moses came to Elizabeth, took her hand, and bowed. "May I have this dance, my Lady?"

"Of course, I would be delighted." As they followed the other dancers around the crowded room, Elizabeth could see all the young couples around them. "Oh, Moses, they look so young."

"Dear Elizabeth, they remind me of you the first day you came aboard the *Lady Catherine*. You just floated from deck to deck. That was the day the Captain fell head over heels in love with you."

"Moses, you're too kind. You're correct; I have wonderful memories sailing upon the *Lady Catherine*."

All of a sudden, there was a crash and a scream. Elizabeth could see two men fighting. One had the other pinned to the floor, thrashing and banging. She could hear the sound of fists hitting flesh. A young woman was screaming for them to stop.

Moses had already left Elizabeth's side. John Charles, Ed Cook, and Wayne joined Moses. All four were breaking up the fight. They dragged the young men outside, still yelling and kicking.

Everything was quiet. Alexander cleared his voice. "Sorry for the interruption." He then asked everyone to join in dancing with Kate and him. He glanced toward the band. "Can you play Keep on the Sunnyside?"

Moses looked towards Wayne and said, "This is my favorite song. Join me in singing:

> There's a dark and a troubled side of life;
> There's a bright and a sunny side, too;
> Tho' we meet with the darkness and strife,
> The sunny side we also may view.
> [Chorus]
> Keep on the sunny side, always on the sunny side,
> Keep on the sunny side of life;

It will help us every day, it will brighten all the
way,
If we keep on the sunny side of life.
Tho' the storm in its fury break today,
Crushing hopes that we cherished so dear,
Storm and cloud will in time pass away,
The sun again will shine bright and clear.

Let us greet with a song of hope each day,
Tho' the moments be cloudy or fair;
Let us trust in our Savior always,
Who keepeth everyone in His care.[i]

As Moses and Wayne sang their hearts out, Alexander took Kate into his arms and guided her onto the dance floor. They were happy to see others joining them.

"Kate, what happened?" Alexander asked. "Wasn't that Edward on the top?" He smiled as other dance couples glided past him and Kate.

"I'm afraid you're correct. He's my brother. Mother and Father worried that Edward would do something. They were right. He can't go anywhere without starting trouble. Alexander, he won't hurt me; he'll listen to me. I'll go outside and see what I can do."

"Do be careful; I'll see to Mother until you return." They gracefully left the dance floor, Kate hurrying outside, and Alexander headed towards his mother.

Crossing the churchyard, white dress billowing in the wind, Kate found Edward standing alone under the old oak tree. "I'm sorry, Kate. I've ruined your wedding, haven't I?" Edward couldn't meet Kate's eyes.

"What caused you to fight|?"

"Did you know we had cousins in Sober Island?"

"Edward, we have cousins all over the place."

"But I didn't know there were some in Sober Island."

Kate still didn't understand. "Why would that make you fight? Where is the other guy?"

"I don't know, but he told me he is a cousin from Sober Island. Every time I even hear those words, Sober Island, anger burns through me. . ."

*****

Alexander had found his mother, the look of alarm still present. "Alexander, who were those young men? Thank heavens Moses and John Charles were here."

"And Wayne was right in the middle of it. His right hand took hold of the back of the young man's collar and still had him going out the front door."

"Wasn't that Kate's father helping out?"

"One of the young men was Edward, Kate's brother. He can be a hothead at times. Kate went out to see what she could do. He seems to listen to her."

"I'm sorry he had to ruin your wedding!" It was Maude. She had walked over to talk to Alexander and Elizabeth.

"It's okay, Maude. No harm done. Moses, John Charles, and Wayne were able to control him."

"No one can handle him!" Maude retorted. "He is going to get in big trouble one of these days. He's not welcome at our home anymore. And he knows it. Where is Kate?"

"She went to see if she could help outside. She seemed to think she could make a difference." In Alexander's mind, he was not sure she could.

"Kate spoils him. Always has."

Elizabeth saw Kate coming towards them. "Here she comes now."

Alexander came to her side. "How are things?"

"Fine, things are fine now. Father is taking him home."

"What about the other guy?"

"Moses and John Charles are taking care of Ralph now."

"Who is he?" Alexander did not know him.

"Ralph is a cousin of mine. He was over from Sober Island and decided he would come to the wedding. I haven't seen him in years. He apologized to me and asked me to tell you he was sorry for what took place."

"What started the fight? What caused Edward to be so angry?"

"That's the funny thing," Kate said. "Ralph said Edward threw the first punch after he answered his question of where he was from. All he said was Sober Island, and he felt Edward's fist on his jaw."

"As Father took him away, all I heard Edward say over and over again was 'nothing good comes from Sober Island'."

Chapter Eight

A Peddler Among Us

Alexander pushed through the crowd of young men standing just outside the post office. In Sheet Harbour, six young men is a crowd. As for the post office, it really wasn't a post office at all. It was Bob Hall's place; however, everyone in Sheet Harbour, Mushaboom, and Watt Section called it the post office.

Bob Hall was a famous person around these parts. Everyone knew that William (Bob) Hall became the first postmaster in Sheet Harbour. It was official from the provincial government back in May of 1873. That was twenty-seven years ago. Now it was 1900 and Bob Hall's place was a meeting area, especially minutes before the stagecoach was to arrive from Halifax.

The people of Sheet Harbour thought they were very lucky to have Norman Stewart, for without Norman there would be no stagecoach. He made the run once a day beginning in Halifax and ended his journey at Moser River. The next morning, he would rise early to make the run back to Halifax.

What a sight to see on a fine evening in summer. Down the long, straight, stretch in a cloud of dust, came Norman, holding back on the reins. His prancing pair of greys was magnificent, eyes flashing, nostrils distended, and tails high. When the dust cleared, out from the bumping coach would step a tired travelling salesman or two, or someone discharged from the hospital in Halifax. Nevertheless, what everyone was waiting for today was the mail, which included Halifax newspapers.

People gathered in front of Bob Hall's place until the summer ended when fall turned into winter with the first snow. Then the mail arrived in Sheet Harbour by a packet boat. Depending on the winter weather, one never knew when the mail would arrive.

Alexander was here to mail a letter to Moses from his mother, Elizabeth. Plus, of course, to see if a letter had arrived from the previous week, for Moses and Elizabeth corresponded often.

"You must be expecting Norman anytime now."

"Anytime," Bob replied. "I can see the dust rising over there letting me know. . . Look!" Bob pointed his finger out the window. Across the harbour, a dust cloud was forming. "He's coming now. Be here in fifteen minutes or so, depending on how tired his greys are."

More people gathered out front. They had seen the dust cloud also. It was a festive feeling in the air. Who was going to step out of the coach today?

The greys didn't look tired to Alexander. The beautiful animals seemed to know they were important to everyone standing there greeting them when they arrived. They pranced, snorted, and gave a good show.

Norman threw two leather bags and a small worn suitcase to the young men standing below. He then jumped down and, before greeting the people, he went to the front of the coach. Placing his hand in his pocket, he retrieved two lumps of sugar. He talked softly to each horse. "Good boy." He placed the sugar between his lips. "Good girl." She opened her teeth to take the sugar. Norman always took care of his horses first.

"Did you have a good trip?" Alexander stepped forward to shake Norman's hand.

"Running a little late this evening. Made my stop in Clam Harbour. Found old Isaac sick as a dog. Couldn't even speak. Gotten himself out of bed just to meet the stage."

"Anything serious?" Alexander knew Isaac; everyone on the eastern shore of Nova Scotia knew Isaac.

"His quinsy[ii] is acting up again. He has been in bed for a week."

"That quinsy can be nasty stuff."

"His woman makes him gargle with Epson salt. Here's the mail." He threw a leather bag in Bob Hall's direction.

The young men swarmed around Bob like bees to honey. "Go on with you. Step aside, no one gets anything until the mail is sorted." Glancing back, he said, "See you tomorrow morning early." His arm rose as a farewell towards Norman.

"I will be on my way now." I will pick the mail up 8 a.m. sharp." Norman made it look easy as he climbed up on the stage.

In a flash, Norman was off. Alexander watched as the pair of greys faded away, rounding the curve towards Lowe's Ferry.

Alexander was so busy talking with Norman that he hadn't noticed the man who had departed the stagecoach. A short, thin man with a funny hat, carrying a carpetbag and some kind of banjo, was standing before the post office. He was alone because all the young men were inside with Bob. The carpetbag must have been heavy, for when he slung it over his shoulder, it made the small guy take two steps forward.

"Charles Asaff is the name." He offered his hand to Alexander as he introduced himself. For a small man, his handshake was like that of a lumberjack, one you would remember.

"Alexander Kenney, glad to meet you, Charles."

Charles rearranged his carpetbag and the instrument Alexander thought was a banjo. "Alexander, now that I'm in Sheet Harbour, where should I start?" Charles looked right then left.

"If you go left," Alexander was following Charles's gaze, "Conrod House Hotel, and a few shops."

"And if I go right?"

"You go far enough, it will be Watt Section and the fishing wharf."

Charles was deep in thought.

"What do you have in that carpet bag?"

Charles adjusted the heavy load. "Everything." Charles' eyes lit up like candles. "I have beautiful things for the ladies, and things for the gentlemen, they cannot live without."

"I'm headed towards Watt Section myself. I'll give you a lift if you like. That is my wagon over there." Alexander turned his head towards old Black Beauty. He was old, but still able to pull the small wagon.

"Thanks. Maybe you could introduce me to the fishermen. They may be in need of something in here." Charles patted his carpetbag.

"I believe my mother would like to see what is in there. Also, she would enjoy your company. Wait here, I will see if there is a letter waiting for me."

Black Beauty knew the routine well; he was on his way to the ferry. As Black Beauty stepped upon the wooden ferry, his hooves made a racket that indicated how large of a horse he was. The trip to the ferry gave the peddler and Alexander time to get acquainted.

"Any mail, Alexander?" Elbridge Lowe always spoke to his riding customers.

"Two letters for Mother and a newspaper for me."

"I can see Elizabeth sitting in the parlour this very evening reading stories from Moses."

"You're quite right, she will save this letter for this evening."

"And who is your passenger?"

"I'm so sorry, I should have introduced him sooner." Alexander turned to Charles. "This is Charles. I'm sorry, what was your name again?"

"Charles Asaff."

"Yes, Charles Asaff." Turning to Elbridge, "He was just telling me he's originally from Mount Lebanon in Syria. Do you know where Syria is, Elbridge?"

"Can't say that I do? Not here in Nova Scotia, is it?"

Alexander laughed. "No, not here in Nova Scotia." Alexander flung his right arm out towards the ocean. "All the way to the other side of the ocean."

Now it was Charles' turn to laugh. He was impressed that Alexander knew where Syria was. Not many people did. "Nice to meet you, Elbridge, my family lives in Halifax now."

"Did you know, Elbridge, Nova Scotia is five times larger than Mount Lebanon in Syria?" Alexander knew his geography well, thanks to his father, Heman.

"Mount Lebanon in Syria cannot be very big. After all, Nova Scotia is one of the smallest provinces in Canada."

"No place to stretch out in Syria," Charles continued. "Love the wide open space here. And the trees, so many trees."

"Taking him home to Mother. He has a carpetbag full of things to sell. And do you see that banjo? It must make some kind of music."

"Not a banjo, Alexander, it's an oud.[iii] But you're correct, it makes sweet music."

"An oud you say, well I never. Did you hear that, Alexander? It's an oud." Elbridge laughed aloud. "I'm sure my Misses would like to have you visit. Stop by the house on your way back."

Alexander was handing over the coins for crossing. Two nickels were in his opened hand. "One nickel will be fine. A free trip for you, Charles, and welcome to Sheet Harbour."

Beauty knew his way home. Alexander and Charles just had to sit and visit. By the time Beauty entered the laneway and rounded the well, Alexander had learned a whole lot more about this man Charles and Syria.

Charles told him there were so many people in Syria that the land was taken. There was no chance to buy any land. There was no work because of the European industrial revolution and the opening of the Suez Canal in 1869, which dried up all of Syria's trade. To make a life for himself and his family, he brought them to Canada. He ended up in Nova Scotia.

Kate opened the door to the blue-shingled cottage. Realizing they had company, she raised her hand to straighten her hair and then took the bottom of her apron to her face to wipe any signs of flour that might be resting there.

"Kate, this is Charles Asaff. He arrived on the stage from Halifax. We will be the first ones to see what he has there in that carpet bag."

"Welcome, Charles. Come in the kitchen, you must be hungry after your journey. I just made bread. Would you like a sandwich?"

"I would," Alexander answered first.

Meanwhile, Charles thought this was a good beginning of his trip. Maybe he would make money today and get food too.

"Alexander, you take care of Beauty. Charles, come this way to the kitchen." Kate led the way. "Mother," she raised her voice, "we have company." Then turning to Charles, "You can sit right here at the table. Make yourself at home."

"All I have is molasses and fresh butter. And I believe the bread is done." Kate used her apron as an oven mitt to take, not one loaf of hot bread from the oven, but four. "Nothing like hot bread from the oven. You arrived just in time, Charles. Mother, do you want a piece of bread?"

Elizabeth was standing at the doorway to the kitchen. She moved slowly these days, but nothing would keep her away from fresh bread, and company topped it off.

"Come sit in the rocking chair by the stove. We don't want you to take a chill."

"Don't fuss so, Kate. It's still summer. I will not take a chill."

"That sea breeze makes it feel like fall. Look, Charles has a warm jacket."

"Ma'am, don't mind me. I've been cold since I got off the boat a month ago. I'm from a warmer climate, but I enjoy the fresh air. Every breath you take cleans out your lungs."

"Never thought of it that way," replied Kate.

"Heman loved the salt air," Elizabeth continued. "He always said he would bottle it and bring it back to me. That is when we lived in Halifax. Kate, the air was full of coal dust. Everybody had coal, and it was very messy."

"I'm afraid the air is still that way in Halifax. That's why my family lives just outside the city. Closer to a park they call Point Pleasant."

"Oh, Point Pleasant Park. One of the first times I met Heman, we went there." Elizabeth's mind slid back in time, and she smiled.

The kitchen door opened and in marched Alexander. "Is that bread cool enough to eat? I'm hungry as a bear."

"Come sit down with us, Alexander." Kate enjoyed taking care of her new husband.

As the evening progressed, darkness settled over Watt Section. They could hear the rhythm of the ocean in the background. Each wave took its turn rolling upon the rocks. Looking out the window of the parlour, Kate could see that the lighthouse was doing her job of sending her light out upon the vast ocean.

It was a bright night. Millions of stars twinkled overhead. There was no need for the foghorn. The ships could see Watt Light many miles out to sea.

Elizabeth sat in her upright upholstered chair. There was a hurricane lamp on a small table sitting on a pink and white doily. It gave off just enough light for Elizabeth to read her letters. Her letters wouldn't be read that night. However, she didn't mind, for Charles sat close to the coffee table setting up his wares.

Alexander smiled at what he saw before him. Both his mother and Kate sat on the edge of their seats waiting for the show to begin. Kate had three additional lamps lit tonight to make sure everyone could see. Charles began unrolling a heavy, coloured cloth, revealing its treasures. There were sewing accessories. Spools of coloured thread, pins, needles, measuring tapes, thimbles, and elastic also lay there. Then he brought out his fabrics. That's when Elizabeth couldn't help but ooh and aah. She knew a good fabric when she saw it. Her father would be proud of her.

It didn't take long for Kate and Elizabeth to pick out material for new dresses. Naturally, Alexander had to give his opinion of what he liked best.

Charles saved the best for last. He brought from his carpetbag jewelry, perfumes, lace, and knitted shawls. So many things to choose from. At last, they decided on a

Figure 21: Alexander Hugh Kenney and Catherine Deborah Cook Kenney

Figure 22: Back Row from left to right: Sadie, Catherine (Kate), Alexander. Front Row: Left to right: Pearl (Gerald's wife), Gerald, Bertha, Erna, Elbridge (my father). Missing: Lloyd, Merle, Hazel, Basil.

Figure 23: The cottage built by Captain Heman Godfrey Kenney after the Show House burned. This is where Alexander and Catherine raised their family.

Figure 24: Sarah (Leslie) Ann Conrod. She and her husband, Theodore Conrod, from Leslie Bay acquired the hotel at West River, and he and his wife, Sarah Ann (Leslie) ran it for years. They called it the "Conrod House."

Figure 25: The Conrod House Hotel became the "MacDonald House" in 1926.

Figure 26: Church: Saint James United Church of Canada.

Figure 27: Community of Sheet Harbour at this time.

Figure 28: Cook Road where Maude, Catherine, and Edward grew up.

Figure 29: The Chedabucto (Chebucto) was one of the coasters that delivered mail throughout the province.

Figure 30: Captain Heman Godfrey Kenney

Figure 31: Dance Hall in Cook Settlement

Figure 32: East River Bridge being built to take the place of Elbridge Lowes' Ferry.

Figure 33: East River Mill

Figure 34: Houses in community of Sheet Harbour

Figure 35: Houses in the community of Sheet Harbour. Home of John Angus MacPhee.

Figure 36: Houses in community of Sheet Harbour

Figure 37: Winslow Kenney, husband of Maude.

Figure 38: Location of Watt Light House

Figure 39: Another Mill in Sheet Harbour

Figure 40: *The Marlis*

Figure 41: *S. S. Dufferin*

Figure 42: West River Wharf Sheet Harbour

Figure 43: A Wharf in Sheet Harbour

small bottle of perfume and a brooch with a pearl resting in a flower for Kate. Elizabeth chose lace, for she could tell it was beautifully made.

"Now it's your turn." Charles turned to Alexander and began opening another roll of material. Alexander could see suspenders, shoelaces, shaving brushes and blades with wooden carved handles.

"I could always use a new shaving brush." He reached to test the bristles, not too stiff and not too soft. He found just the one for him.

"And now to thank you, I will leave you with a song. My oud please."

"Your oud?" Elizabeth never heard that word before.

"His instrument, Mother. It's not a banjo."

"I knew it didn't look like a banjo."

"It's more like a pear-shaped guitar that has a very long neck." Alexander passed the instrument to Charles. Charles made sweet music from his oud. They listened to the music for a long time. They didn't have the opportunity to hear beautiful music very often. However, good things must always come to an end. It was late and Charles said he must leave.

"Where will you stay this evening?" Alexander asked.

"I noticed your barn. Would it inconvenience you any, if I made my bed there?"

"No, not at all. I will call Wayne, he will see you settled."

Wayne didn't like peddlers; he didn't trust them. This Charles Asaff from Syria he trusted even less. He made it clear to Mr. Asaff that he would be watching him closely.

Charles was used to people treating him badly. He didn't blame them, for many peddlers from his home country were crooks. Charles had to live down a reputation, for all Syrian men were deceitful by habit. Everyone knew they lied most naturally by preference and would only tell the truth when it would serve their purpose best.

He could tell Wayne had heard about them. However, Charles would do no harm to the Kenneys, for they had accepted him, and he felt welcomed in their home. Nevertheless, he would leave early in the morning as Wayne requested.

*****

The next evening, Charles found himself at the Conrod House Hotel. The owner, Leslie Conrod, bought the last of his wares. Now he would return to Halifax earlier than planned. However, he would be back, for this was a good route for a salesman like himself.

The last night in Sheet Harbour, he would celebrate. His oud always made an instant party. Those that gathered at the hotel were ready to party. Everyone was dancing, laughing, and singing. The atmosphere was happy. Charles liked Sheet Harbour.

It wasn't long after he was thinking this that a dark shadow seemed to fill the room. Everyone looked towards the doorway. A young man was standing there. At first, Charles believed he came to join the party, but everyone dancing just stopped and moved away from the center of the room.

Leslie Conrod met the young man at the door. The young man left, slamming the door behind him. Nevertheless, the damage was done. Everyone just drifted away.

"Sorry, Charles."

"What has happened? Who was that young man? Did he not want to join the party?"

"Edward Cook wouldn't know how to party. He is trouble. We were lucky tonight he decided to leave. He accomplished what he came to do. Look around. No one is partying now."

Chapter Nine

Strong As an Ox

Edward Cook had nothing good to say about Sheet Harbour. Just because he was raised there didn't mean he would have to like it. Raised there by a man who wasn't his father, and a woman who wasn't his mother. His mother was dead. Plus, those girls were not his sisters. Kate had been the only one who had cared. Kate had been the only one he could talk to or wanted to talk to. Now, Kate didn't have any time for him. She had gone on with her life. Married that Kenney. Lived way down in Watt Section. She may as well be a hundred miles away.

I think it's funny, when I enter a room, everything stops. Just like back there at the hotel. Everyone was dancing until they saw me. Power. I have power over this place. They know not to mess with me. A good fight. That's what I'm good for. They were lucky I didn't feel like fighting. Not tonight."

"I saw the skinny guy playing the music. He looked like a foreigner. What was he playing? Never heard music like that. Doesn't matter. I made him stop too. Nobody deserves to be happy. Not when I'm around.

That's okay. I'll go on with my life. Move on as they say. Good riddance to them all. Except for Kate. I'll carry her in my heart. But I'm leaving. I'll start a new life where no one knows me. Where no one knows my path. I have to get out of here. But, where do I go? Halifax? That's a big city. I could lose myself in a city like that. What about Truro? That's a better idea. Truro would be away from the ocean. That's what I need. Get away from the ocean. I hate the ocean. I could go along the trail to Truro. There are always wagons going that way. I could get a ride to Truro. And that's just what Edward Cook did.

Two days later, he was walking down Main Street, Truro. Truro was situated at the head of the Salmon River, near the entrance to the Cobequid Bay. The area around Truro was originally called 'Wagobagitik' by the local Mi'kmaq inhabitants. The name has been interpreted as meaning 'end of the water flow' or 'the bay runs far up', in reference to the world's highest tides rising up from the Bay of Fundy. On the edge of town, visitors flock to the Salmon River to view the tidal bore that occurs twice a day because of the immense incoming Fundy tide. Acadian settlers, arriving in the early 1700s, transformed that name into Cobequid. It wasn't until after the expulsion of the Acadians that settlers of Scots-Irish descent named the town after the city of Truro in Cornwall, England.

You may think Edward was a very smart man, knowing all the history of Truro. Except he had just learned it all, on the way to Truro from Sheet Harbour. The wagon which stopped to pick him up had a very friendly driver. Ken McGinnis and his son Brian. They were from Truro, heading back from Middle Muscodobit. They knew a farmer there who gave them a great deal on a planting machine. Anything to help the farming their family did just outside Truro in Bible Hill. Three generations of the McGinnis family had farmed the same land. They were very proud people and knew the history of the area well. Edward learned a lot about Truro.

Edward also learned that Truro had always been an important junction for travelers in Nova Scotia. The town's importance increased dramatically with the construction of the Nova Scotia Railway between Halifax and Pictou in 1858. The Intercolonial Railway came in 1872, making a connection to the Annapolis Valley's Dominion Atlantic Railway. Truro became a hub not just for goods and passengers but for industry as well, such as the Truro Woolen Mills. Then Ken, who was telling Edward story after story, got very quiet. *I guess that was all there was to tell* thought Edward. Edward remembered every word. This was his new home, and he wanted to know all there was to know.

"Where do you think I should start looking for work?" Edward broke the silence.

"The railroad." That was the first time Brian spoke. "The railroad is always looking for men. Strong men and you look strong."

Ken smiled at his son. "He wants to work on the railroad. Wants to leave the farm, he does. But it will be a few years yet before I let him go out on his own."

Edward looked at Brian, "That is where I will start then, the railroad."

*****

Spring had come early. The farmers had planted their fields, not that Edward would have noticed. He didn't notice the plants sticking their heads out of the soil, reaching for the warm sun. All of his attention went to the 'round house' where he was now working. Brian was right; they were hiring at the railroad. Edward was proof of that. All of this was new to Edward and he liked it. He started as a railcar repairman, and in a few short weeks from now, he would move up to assistant signal worker. His boss, G.G. Murphy, was a strict man. He watched his workers like a hawk. However, he also was a fair man. Edward was told by his fellow workers, "If you kept your nose clean, you'll succeed in the railroad business."

G.G. Murphy, not only worked for the railroad, he owned and worked a very large farm over in Bible Hill. His corn plants were also breaking through the ground, reaching for the sun. Murphy didn't just live in Bible Hill, a growing community on the north side of Salmon River just opposite Truro. He was a prominent and a well-known citizen. He, his father, and grandfather before him helped build the town to what it was today. Down on the main street, there was a courthouse and a Masonic Hall of which he was the Field Operations Supervisor of all the deacons of the group. There were two inns, and ten years ago, the Nova Scotia Agricultural College had been established. He was well known, but all Murphy really cared about was his family. His wife, Alice, and his daughter, Rosemary, meant the world to him.

Edward had caught glimpses of Rosemary when she helped her father in his office at the rail yard. Just one glance at her, and he had to stop whatever he was doing and just watch her. Of course, his fellow workers noticed and teased him. However, this teasing didn't bother Edward at all. He had changed.

Edward had the opportunity to meet her. Murphy invited all his workers to Bible Hill for a community dance that was held at the Masonic Hall. Oh, how he liked Rosemary. Since then he had been invited to her home. Life was good in Truro.

*****

Kate and Alexander were relaxing in the parlour after a day of chores that never seemed to end. Elizabeth was in her room, sitting by her window, staring at the lighthouse.

"Is your mother alright?" Kate asked Alexander.

"Yes, I believe so. Why do you ask?"

"I worry about her sitting there looking beyond that lighthouse. She spends a lot of time doing that."

"She misses Father. They had a wonderful relationship, those two did. Just like I want us to have." Alexander reached for Kate. "Now we have little ones running around this house. Three of them, Kate. Father would have been proud. It's sad that Lloyd, Hazel, and Erna will never know my father."

"Don't forget, another one to be born soon." Kate enjoyed the time she could be alone with Alexander. This was her favourite time of day. Supper was finished and cleaned up, the children were in bed, and her mother-in-law was always in her room looking out her window.

"How can I forget?" Alexander replied. "We may not be successful in a lot of things, but it seems we're good at making babies."

"We don't talk about such things, Alexander." Kate couldn't help smiling but quickly changed the subject back to his father.

"You and Mother can tell our children all about the great Captain Heman and the *Lady Catherine*. I never met him, but I already feel like I have always known him because you and your mother speak of him often. Everyone in Sheet Harbour knew of him. My father talked of him. Said he was a great man."

"You would have liked him," Alexander continued, "but he was always away on the *Lady Catherine*. Being a schooner captain, he spent long periods of time away from home."

Kate picked up a letter and began to open it.

"A letter?" Alexander hadn't noticed it lying on a doily on the small table beside the settee.

"Yes, Wayne picked up the mail and this was waiting for me." She held the paper up for Alexander to see.

"From Edward?" Alexander raised his eyebrow. "He's been missing for months. Not that I've missed him. I'm sorry, Kate."

"Now, Alexander, he is my brother."

"You're right. Now, why do you have a letter from Edward?"

"He's in Truro. He begins by saying he's sorry he didn't say goodbye."

"Truro? What's he doing in Truro?"

"You're not going to believe it, but he says he's found a girl, Rosemary Murphy."

"You're right. I don't believe it. He was in trouble so often. I felt sorry for your parents."

"Edward had it hard. You know he had a black mark on him since he was a child. He's never been able to handle his mother committing suicide, and also the reason for it."

"That would be hard. But now you say he has found a girl in Truro."

"Yes, he's working with her father at the Canadian Pacific Railway."

"Good for him."

"Let's hope so. But I still worry about him."

"Did you hear that Maude and John Winslow are opening a store just up over the hill from the graveyard?" Alexander was ready to change to another subject. Anything but Edward.

"No, I didn't. I don't hear anything about anyone living here. I'm so isolated from everyone else."

"Don't you like living here?"

"Of course, I do. But without your mother around I would be lonely."

"There's the children. You've kept busy with them."

"Yes, but it's nice to have an adult to talk to. I love our children, Alexander, and the children to come." She looked down at her expanding waistline.

*****

Maude and John Winslow were busy stocking shelves. It was almost the end of summer. There was a light frost on the pumpkins, and the sugar maples had a tint of red, just a tease of the brilliance of colour that would soon come.

"You know, John, I believe we could buy vegetables from the locals. Their gardens are coming in nicely now. We could grow our own out back next year. Wouldn't vegetables look nice in a barrel over there in the corner? Maybe we could get some fabric and place it in that corner. We could use that table over there. I just know the ladies around here would buy it. And. . ."

"Whoa, just a minute, Maude." John was shaking his head. "I'm happy you are enjoying working in this store, but you must think things through, my dear. First, why would the locals sell us their vegetables and have to buy them back from us? No one is going to buy vegetables here if they have vegetables in their own backyard."

"Oh, I do see what you mean." Maude placed another can of beans on the shelf.

"But I do like the idea of fabric and we could use that table. We would have to sell it cheaper than the peddlers." John was deep in thought. "I don't think it would be worth it. Let's stay with flour, sugar, canned goods, and nails. Things the peddlers cannot carry."

"You're probably right. You're smart, John." She smiled and took her apron, wiped her hands, more from habit than the need to clean her hands. "I need to tend to the children. Roy is a good helper now, and he is good at watching Violet and Jean. But I don't dare leave the children for long."

Maude went up the stairs and opened a wooden door that led to their living space. There were four rooms on the second floor. A kitchen with a small cook stove, a wooden table with four mismatched chairs sat under the window. The view from the window was beautiful. Being up on this hill, they could see all the way out of Sheet Harbour Passage and to the ocean beyond. The blues of the sky and the ocean ran together towards the horizon. Once when Maude was drinking her tea, she saw a whale come up for air, blasting a stream of water above its head, before it sank back under the blue water. Maude no longer had time to sit and look out the window, for now, she had a store and her family to take care of. However, she sure did enjoy the rocking chair given to her by her grandmother. It was beside the stove and just in front of the washbasin. Her grandmother's picture was hung above the washbasin, beside the towel rack. Every time Maude dried her hands, she could see her grandmother's picture. She was going to be just like her, for Grandmother Cook was a strong woman. When she set her mind to do something, it always got done.

There were two small rooms off the stair landing. They were just right for bedrooms. One for her and John, and one for the children. Her bedroom had room for two chairs, one on each side of the bed. The children's room had a homemade baby bed and two small cots for Roy and Violet. This is also where the children played.

Maude took several minutes tending to her children. She wished she had more time to spend with them, but John needed her help. Maude heard the kitchen door open.

"Maude, Maude, are you in here?"

Well, of course, I am, where else would I be? "In here John."

"Maude, you have company."

Maude quickly placed Baby Jean in her bed, took her apron, wiped her hands, and started into the kitchen. Roy and Violet were right at her heels following her. A large smile filled Maude's face. "Kate, it's you. It's been a long time. Come sit down at the table."

Kate had her own children at her heels. Maude's large smile was contagious, for Kate came forward and hugged her sister. "Yes, it does seem forever. Alexander had to make a trip up West River and to the post office. He suggested he drop us off here for a visit."

"Look at him." Maude looked more closely at her nephew Lloyd. "Look how much you have grown. He looks more like Alexander every day. And look at the two girls." Maude bent down to Hazel and Erna's level. "Who do you look like?"

"Grandmother Elizabeth." Hazel was quick to reply. Erna was hiding behind her mother's skirt.

Violet was jumping up and down. "Auntie Kate, Auntie Kate."

"How is my favourite girl? And your sister, where have you put your sister?"

Roy was pleased to enter into the conversation. "This way, Auntie Kate, this way." He took Kate's hand and led her into the bedroom. Kate picked up Baby Jean and danced around the room.

"That's enough now, children." Maude looked at Kate. "You shouldn't be dancing around, not in your condition. How have you been feeling?"

"Fine, I feel fine. I always feel fine when I'm pregnant."

Maude turned to the children. "Auntie Kate and I have a lot of talking to do. You children stay here and show Baby Jean this book. You can be with Auntie Kate again in a little while."

Kate sat down at the table, while Maude took the tea off the cook stove. It was still warm from breakfast. "I'm sorry I don't have anything baked. We had supplies arrive on the coaster from Halifax. I've been so busy getting it on the shelves that I haven't had time to even think."

"It's okay since I have brought cinnamon rolls." Kate reached into her canvas bag and placed on the table a dozen rolls. "Baked them this morning."

"I thought I could smell something good. My favourite." Maude slid into the chair across from Kate.

"That's why I brought them. Now, how are you doing, Maude? And the store, everyone is talking about the store."

"Happy as a lark. It's easier on John than going into the woods for lumber, and I hated it when he went lobster fishing. I worried the whole time he was out on that ocean. So this is better, we work together."

"Have you seen Father or Mother? I haven't seen them, it seems like ages."

"Father dropped by just recently to see the store."

"He did? And he didn't come to see me?" Kate looked mad.

"He only stayed thirty minutes. He said he didn't have time to go down the hill and around the bend to see you. He did say he would see you at Christmas."

"Christmas?"

"It's only a few months away. John is closing the store for Christmas. Your place is bigger than ours is. We could all meet at your place for Christmas dinner."

"What about Edward?"

Maude placed her teacup down with a clatter. "What about Edward?"

"We have to send a message asking him to come too."

"Kate, Edward has been away for months now. Have you heard from him? Where is he?"

"He's in Truro."

"Truro can keep him. Mother and Father have been doing so much better since he has gone."

"He's our brother," Maude.

"Not really, no."

"The day Father brought him home was the day he became our brother. You don't understand him like I do."

"You always had more patience with him than I did. Here, do you want another cup of tea?" Maude went to the cook stove to get the teapot.

Kate was steaming mad. Her face was getting hotter; she knew she was going to blow her top. Just like a kettle boiling on the cook stove. "You know, Maude, I'm getting pretty tired of you putting our brother down. Just once I wish I could hear you say something nice about him."

"There's nothing good to tell." Maude put the teacup down in front of Kate. John and I have talked about it. We don't want anything to do with him.

Kate got up so fast from the table, she knocked over her teacup. Hot tea went everywhere. Kate didn't care. "If you don't want anything to do with Edward, I don't want to have anything to do with you." Kate was on her way to the children's room, yelling as she went. "Lloyd, Hazel, Erna, get your coats on, we're going home."

"We just got here. Mother, we can't leave now. We haven't finished the story in this book. This book is all about Black Beauty." Lloyd held up the book he was reading to all the children.

"We have a Black Beauty, don't we Mother?" This was Hazel asking.

Kate didn't even answer. "Now put your coats on, we're leaving."

Maude was now right behind Kate in the narrow hallway. "Kate, you can't leave yet. Alexander isn't back to pick you up. I'm sorry, we won't talk about Edward, please come back in the kitchen."

Kate had already made up her mind, and nothing was changing it. "We will walk. Children, are you ready?" Kate was guiding them down the stairs to the store.

"We have to walk all the way home?" Lloyd was amazed. "What about Erna?"

"Just keep moving." Kate was guiding her children like sheep. "I will carry her." She gave Lloyd her canvas bag that she picked up in the kitchen as she passed by. "You carry this."

It wasn't such a bad walk, for it was downhill. They stopped at the gate of the church cemetery to rest. Lloyd and Hazel climbed up and down the gate. Kate was the one who was tired. She placed Erna down on some green grass where a few daisies were growing. It gave time for Kate to think. It was the first time she stood up to her sister Maude. She couldn't help it, for she loved Edward. Edward was her brother and that was that.

Kate and the children had been home for some time. She was in the kitchen making supper when she heard Alexander and the wagon going around the well, heading for the barn. It wasn't but a minute when she heard him open the door. "Did you not take care of Black Beauty?"

"No, Wayne was there and I asked him to do it. Are you okay?" Alexander came closer to Kate. "I stopped at the store to pick you up, but you weren't there. Maude was worried about you. She said you left, walked home, and were upset about Edward."

"That's right. I'm tired of Maude saying bad things about Edward. Enough is enough, no more. She said John and she have given up on Edward. Well, I have given up on Maude."

"That's going to be a hard thing to do." Alexander took Kate in his arms. "She told me the whole family is coming here for Christmas, which means her too."

*****

Edward couldn't believe he missed Sheet Harbour. He had changed his life. Truro was good for him. No one knew, or if they did know, they were good at hiding it. He never spoke of his past.

He had met Rosemary at a dance. He enjoyed dancing with Rosemary. She was pretty, and he liked the way she did her hair. Her eyes were deep pools of blue water, and she had a laugh that reminded him of a dove, but louder. She was easy to talk too, just like Kate.

It was hard working at the railroad. He didn't mind at all. He remembered the first day he came into the yard, he was directed to G.G. Murphy's office. Murphy took one look at him and said he looked strong enough to lift an ox. He probably could. Murphy was Rosemary's father. Edward was getting to know him quite well. Because of him, he wanted to work hard. He didn't talk much to the other men, but they did talk to him. Just the passing of time talk. He really wasn't used to it. It wasn't like that in Sheet Harbour. No one talked to him there.

It was Rosemary who encouraged Edward to write Kate, for Kate was the only member of the family he shared with. When Kate wrote back, he read it to her. Kate spoke about how the family was coming to her place for Christmas. She wanted Edward to come too. It surprised him that he was homesick for Sheet Harbour. Something inside of him was calling to him. After a week of it going round and round in his brain, he decided to go home. Rosemary's father was disappointed when he told him he was going back to Sheet Harbour for a while. 'And leave your job?' Edward could still hear his words. *Disappointment was written all over his face. That's what I've done all my life. Disappoint people. I'm good at it.*

*****

The first week of December was cold and frosty. When Edward arrived back in Sheet Harbour, Flo and Ed Cook were genuinely happy to see him. With his changed mind, he could see they really did care for him. Maybe now he could be thankful for what they tried to do for him all his life.

Edward made a trip to Watt Section. It was cold on the ferry, as he helped pull it over to the other side. The three-inch rope was wet, cold, and slippery, as he used all the strength he had to pull on the rope. Elbridge seemed to be pleased with his effort; however, he didn't say a word and never made eye contact. Edward paid his nickel and stepped off the scow[iv]. He was trying not to allow his mood to change; he was on his way to see Kate.

At the crest of the hill, he noticed a store. Must be Maude's store; Kate had told him about it in her letter. He couldn't help noticing as he passed by that someone pulled the window shade down.

Why does Kate live down here, so far away from anyone? She has more dead neighbours than live ones, he thought as he walked by St. Andrews Cemetery.

By the time he walked up the laneway to the blue-shingled cottage, his mood was changing. All the anger was coming back. He could feel it. *Maybe it was not such a good idea to return to Sheet Harbour. I forgot how much I hate this place.*

His mind came back to the present as the door flew open, taking Edward out of his daydream, and Kate ran to meet him. It was good to see her. His anger was gone, and he enjoyed the meal and the company. In the parlour, he made conversation with both Kate and Elizabeth. Alexander was interested in his work on the railroad. It was a pleasant evening for all.

Edward's anger didn't stay away long. Only two days after his visit with Kate, his mind started to turn over and over. It didn't help that he had no job. The days were long, and the nights drew longer. One evening, Ed took Flo to her sister's home up shore to tend to her. Flo, the only mother Edward had ever known, was always taking care of the sick. Yet Edward had never taken the time to notice how well the people of Sheet Harbour had thought of her. Now he was alone in the house that was never truly his home. Edward walked back and forth in the house like a caged animal. He couldn't take it any longer. He left the house and headed for the Conrod House Hotel in Sheet Harbour.

All he had to do was to go back to Truro. Nothing was stopping him. He regretted coming back, and he envied the men who would be leaving on that very ship moored at the wharf. *That ship will leave this awful town in the morning. They are lucky. How could I ever think I missed this place? Why did I come back?* Still deep in thought, he opened and passed through the double doors of the Conrod Hotel.

Mrs. Conrod was lighting lamps since the darkness was taking over the harbour. Several people were in the dining room.

Edward didn't care that they were already staring at him. He went forward and sat at a table where he could see the whole room. Now, in front of him, he could see those coming and going. He watched as Mrs. Conrod walked toward his table. He noticed how old she was. Seemed like she had worked here forever.

"Hello, Mrs. Conrod, are you going to ask me to leave?"

"Not unless you want to. Haven't seen you around the harbour in a long time. Where have you been?"

"Truro for a while."

"Are you hungry? Supper is being served now. Baked beans and fish chowder."

"Yes, that would be fine."

Mrs. Conrod left his table and, after speaking with a young red-haired girl, joined a table of three. Edward didn't know the two men who were eating. They must have been off the boat from the States. However, the third one looked familiar. Yes, it was that skinny guy he saw the last time he was in here. The one who had been playing the strange music everyone was dancing too.

The young red-haired girl came by his table with his food. As she placed a large bowl of fish chowder and a plate of baked beans before him, he could not help overhearing the conversation at the other table.

"Charles, have you had a good trade run. It's only Thursday. I don't usually see you until Friday."

"Yes, Mrs. Conrod, I sold all my wares."

"All of them?! Where have you been to sell all your wares in so short a time?"

"Sober Island. I traded suspenders, a wool hat, and dry wool mitts to Captain Patrick Murphy for passage on the *Foaming Billow*. I've not been there before. I don't think they've seen many peddlers over there. I stayed at John Henry's house for the night and returned with Murphy this morning."

The only reason Edward didn't choke is that he was about to place a fork full of beans in his mouth. He dropped his fork with a clatter. No one seemed to notice. Edward stared at the fallen fork. He felt the fire rising from somewhere deep inside coming to a boil. He raised his gaze from the fork to the skinny man. This skinny man had been to Sober Island. This skinny man had been at the very house of his beginning, the beginning of his wretched life. Anger had taken over. Fire burned in his eyes.

I will destroy him. I will destroy everything. But, how? I must be calm. He made his mind be calm. *Be calm and then you can destroy him.* Edward stood up and walked towards the table. When everyone looked up towards him, he calmly said, "May I join you?"

Mrs. Conrod was talking about a young woman she met years ago. "I believe her name was Angeline. She was in trouble, she was. She went back to Sober Island, but I never heard from her again. I've always wondered what happened to her."

"Edward, have you had your dessert? Apple pie is cooling by the window. It should be ready to eat now. Would you like a piece?"

"Yes, that would be fine." He looked up into her eyes. Inside his head, all he could hear was *Sober Island. Sober Island. He has come from Sober Island.* Edward was staring at the skinny man.

"And you, Charles, and of course you, gentlemen, would like a piece?" Mrs. Conrod was looking at all four men sitting at the table. "I may as well bring the whole pie to the table." She pushed back her chair. "I'll be back shortly." Slowly, she raised herself from her chair and walked across the room.

Edward thought he might be shaking. *Calm yourself.* He turned to the men he didn't know. "Are you here from the States?"

"Yes, we are," answered the one who wore a grey, knit sweater.

The other, lighting his pipe, replied, "From Boston. Leaving tomorrow on the high tide."

"And you?" Edward continued to stare at the skinny man.

"Charles Asaff is the name. 'You need it, I find it' is my motto." He raised his hand to Edward.

It took a moment for Edward's mind to clear enough to respond with his hand. The fire, the anger was about to spill out of him. He grabbed Charles Asaff's hand, maybe a little too firmly. *Stay calm.* Edward was trying to control himself.

"You're the peddler then?"

"Yes, from Halifax. I travel all along the Eastern Shore."

"My parents live up East River. They've been asking about you. I'm lucky to find you here. When are you leaving?"

"In the morning on the stage."

"They have an order for you."

"What kind of order?" Charles liked the sound of an order.

My parents have an order. I know it's late, but would you come with me to East River? We can walk it in half an hour. It's just before the ferry. Up on Cook Road."

Charles agreed to go with Edward.

"We can talk about it on the way? What do you say? We could eat our pie with these gentlemen, and then we could leave." Edward pulled out his pocket watch. "Twenty minutes to six. You would be back here by 8 p.m. Plenty of time to rest before your early morning stage."

They started out, walking down the road through Sheet Harbour. Edward's heart was pounding. He thought for sure the skinny peddler could hear it, perhaps even see it. However, it was dark with the fog rolling up the harbour. Edward could barely see twenty feet in front of him.

Edward could tell that this peddler was used to walking, since they both walked at a fast clip. As they were passing the turnoff to Indian Road, Edward asked the peddler if he had ever been down there. The peddler replied, "That I have, and the Indians are a different bunch for sure."

Edward agreed. It was a good place to go for a fight. They began cutting through a path in the woods, leaving the harbour behind.

"What kind of order do your parents want?" Charles was interested in knowing.

"All I know is my mother is planning some kind of party. I guess you would know what she might need. I'm not one for partying."

Passing by the United Church and the Church Hall, they turned left onto East River Road. "Cook Road is just up here on the left." Edward couldn't believe his voice was calm. Inside, something dark was boiling, and evil had taken over. He didn't even know who he was anymore. He laughed to himself. He had never known who he was. His mother. His father. Her secret lover. His mother scorned and rejected. His mother ending her life. All on Sober Island. It all took place there. Anger burned inside. He couldn't hold it inside any longer. Someone had to pay. *This skinny peddler is just the one. No one would ever miss him. Peddlers are never missed. Who cares about peddlers?*

Charles Asaff brought Edward out of his trance. "Doesn't look like anyone is home?" They stopped in front of the Cook family home that was covered in darkness. The windows were as dark as Edward's angry heart.

"Stay here," Edward ordered. "I'll go in and check the place out."

Edward opened the door. He lit the lantern, but he already knew the way. He knew where he was going. Ed had a desk. He opened the second drawer of Ed's desk. The lantern lit up the silver plate on the barrel of the gun that was just lying there. Edward reached for a small leather bag, loosening the string at the top. Two bullets spilled out onto his waiting hand. He quickly loaded the pistol and placed it in his pocket.

"They left a note," Edward yelled to the peddler. He picked up the axe that was standing by the garden gate. He carried the lantern, which gave off a yellow glow in the foggy air. "They're down at my grandparents' house playing cards just down the hill."

The peddler led the way back down the hill from which they came. Edward knew just where he would do it. He counted to fifty and stopped. *Right here, nice tall bushes. Right here. Right now!*

Edward held up the lantern with his left hand, while the right hand went into his pocket. As the glow from the lantern illuminated the evil grin twisted on his face, he raised the pistol, pulled the trigger, and shot the peddler in the back of the head. Dead. Edward set the lantern down. There was plenty of light to see that his aim hit the mark, but, for good measure, he brought the axe up and let it fall. Charles Asaff was gone. The peddler's eyes were staring straight up. Charles Asaff didn't know what hit him. Edward looked up and watched the clouds pass by, going out to sea. He emptied the peddler's pockets and, without even looking, he took a wallet and stuffed it into his own pocket. He then picked the peddler up and raised him above his head. *Strong enough to lift an ox.* With a grunt, a low roar and, with all the strength he had, he threw the body into the tall bushes. He wasn't finished yet. Taking the blood soaked axe, he cut branches from the huge fir tree. He placed the branches carefully over the body. Picking up the lantern, he raised it high. Not even a broken blade of grass could be seen. *No one will even notice,* thought Edward. He was sweating now. He turned around and looked at the darkened house. Something inside him told him to say goodbye. Good-bye to everything in Sheet Harbour. Good-bye. Edward began walking towards Truro.

Chapter Ten

All Together – But One

They're here! They are here!" Elizabeth was basting the largest turkey she had ever seen. "Children, children, take your toys." She was clapping her hands. The children listened better when she clapped her hands. "Put your presents under the Christmas tree."

Santa Claus had arrived the night before, leaving goodies for all the children. Alexander and Kate both loved Christmas. For that matter, so did Elizabeth. She and Heman had passed the joy of Christmas down to Alexander and all their children. Just last night, Christmas Eve, Erna, Lloyd, and Hazel found the largest stocking they could find. They found their spot in the den to place their stocking on since they didn't have a fireplace. Erna placed hers on one end of the chesterfield; Hazel placed hers on the other end. Lloyd placed his on his grandmother's rocking chair. After the children were asleep, it was time for Alexander, Kate, and Elizabeth to cast their magic. An orange was the first thing to be placed in the toe of the stocking. Then they had nuts, bright-coloured ribbon candy, hair clip and comb for the girls, and socks and mittens for Lloyd. To top them off, red grapes hung over the opening of the stockings. For the girls, Santa left two dolls, one with dark hair, one with light hair. Grandmother Elizabeth spent many hours making clothes for each doll. Wayne made beds and surprised everyone when he carried in the dollhouse with tiny furniture for each room. Lloyd got a brand new sled, a pair of skates, and a set of soldiers. When everything was in place, they stood back and admired everything. More than once they proclaimed, "This is the best Christmas we've had yet."

The toys and the children were lying everywhere. Elizabeth clapped her hands again. It didn't take long for them to place everything back under the tree.

"Kate, Alexander, our company is here. They're stopping at the well." Elizabeth was back in the kitchen and could see out the window of the back door. Snow was falling like rose petals, large rose petals floating towards the ground. They were not yellow or red, but white, large white rose petals.

"Alexander, you may need to sweep the doorstep. The door may not open." Just as she was speaking, she could see a large man's form pass by the window with a broom tucked under his armpit and sweeping back and forth, causing the snow-like petals to fly first to one side of the doorstep and then the other. "Wayne." The familiar name came from Elizabeth's lips. Wayne always took care of the things that needed to be done, even before anyone spoke of them. "Alexander, where are you, dear? I need help putting this huge turkey back in the oven. This turkey is so large it may take two men. Alexander, they are stepping out of their sleigh."

Alexander arrived through the doorway between the dining room and the kitchen. His head hit the mistletoe that Kate had hung there. There was no one to kiss, but that didn't occur to him, for he was in a hurry. His hand reached up and made the mistletoe stop swinging as he passed through. "Mother, are you okay?"

"Now that you're here, I'll be fine. See." She pointed towards the window in the back door.

Alexander tried to look where her finger pointed. He had to look between the children jumping up and down, for they had returned from the den, and they were looking out the window of the back door. Alexander could see people retrieving packages from the sleigh. Then another sleigh came up on the other side of the well. He could hear the ringing of the sleigh bells and a loud 'WHOA' as the two horses came to a stop. Steam was coming out of the horses' nostrils, as they pranced and threw their heads side to side. Alexander knew happy horses when he saw them, and these were happy horses.

Kate was now standing in the doorway between the dining room and kitchen. Alexander couldn't help noticing she was under the mistletoe.

"The family is arriving!" Kate's eyes were shining.

Alexander took the opportunity to take the four steps that separated them and kissed her. "Merry Christmas, dear."

Kate laughed. "Thank you, dear, but don't you think you should welcome our guests?"

"Enough, you two." Elizabeth broke into their private moment. "Alexander, get this turkey back into the oven. It won't be done before dinner."

"Yes, Mother." Alexander not only could smell the turkey, but also the potato dressing that was stuffed inside. "Smells good," he said, as he quickly placed homemade, red oven mitts on his hands, took hold of the large roasting pan, and hoisted. "Open the oven, Mother, this thing is heavy."

"Smells wonderful!" Kate was on her way to the back door. "Erna, put your coat on." As the door opened, Erna flew outside. Kate took a heavy shawl off the pegged wall and wrapped it around her shoulders. Opening the door, she cried, "Merry Christmas. Welcome to all."

Alexander was right behind her. "Here comes another sleigh!" He pointed to the entrance of the laneway. "Everyone has arrived at the same time." Cousins were greeting cousins, and all the children were running around the well, trying to catch the snowflakes with their tongues as they floated to the ground. "Watch out for the sleigh!" Alexander didn't want to lose any children on this wonderful Christmas Day.

Elizabeth remained standing by the stove. She could hear all the ruckus and decided it was safer for her to stay where she was. *What are we going to do with all the coats and boots?* she thought to herself.

Alexander was shouting orders, as he laid newspapers down along the wall by the back door. "Place your boots here."

"Lloyd, come here." Lloyd answered the call and was now standing beside his father. "Take their coats and wraps and put them on Grandmother's bed." He glanced towards his mother. Elizabeth nodded in agreement. This was the normal custom since her bedroom was the only one on the main floor.

The line began. The entrance by the back door was a small space for so many people; however, anyone living in Nova Scotia in the wintertime knew this and understood the procedure. The first ones to arrive were the first ones to come through the door.

Alexander turned and saw Hazel standing watching from the corner of the room. "Hazel, get your Grandmother Flo a chair from the kitchen. She needs to sit to take off her boots."

"Yes, Father." Hazel was two years younger than Lloyd but one year older than Erna. She thought Lloyd got to do everything. She just knew she was big enough to do anything Lloyd did. She was delighted that her father asked her to get a chair.

"Thank you, Hazel. You're such a big girl." Hazel liked Grandmother Flo; she liked the way she talked and she smelled good, like one smells after a bath. Flo shook her wool coat over the newspapers on the floor. Snow had accumulated on the collar and shoulders of Flo's wool coat. Lloyd was ready to take her coat and Grandfather Ed's. He headed for the back bedroom, passing through the dining room and through the hallway to a doorway on the left just below the staircase. Lloyd's favourite time of the year, Christmas. He couldn't help looking to the right into the den, where the biggest Christmas tree they ever had stood at attention. Father and Mother, Uncle Wayne, and, of course, his sisters, took the sleigh and Beauty, and cut down this beautiful fir tree just a week ago. It was so much fun. Mother helped make the decorations. There were large red and yellow flowers made from tissue paper. Then, of course, the children helped string cranberries and popcorn. Grandmother Elizabeth brought out a box full of decorations. Each one had a story to tell. Grandfather Heman had brought them back from trade routes he had made on his schooner the *Lady Catherine*. There were glass reindeer pulling a sleigh where Santa was sitting holding his bag of toys. They were bought in New Orleans. They had a special place on the pump organ, sitting on fir branches with a lovely red satin bow.

"Lloyd, where are you? Did you get lost?" It was Alexander coming down the hallway with a very large load of coats.

"Sorry, Father, I'm right here. Are there any other coats to bring?"

"The children are still playing outside. When they come in, their coats can be hung on the pegs by the back door. You and Hazel can collect chairs from the dining room and put them in the den. Our company is headed that way."

The kitchen was full of women. At least that is what Elizabeth thought. Kate and her sister, Maude, were peeling potatoes, carrots, turnips, and parsnips. Wayne had made several trips to the cellar just the night before. Thanks to their garden, the vegetable bins were full and would last them all winter. Elizabeth was happy to have Mary Elizabeth, her first-born, and her other daughters, Eliza, Laura, and Sarah, finishing the pie crust on both the apple and cherry pies. Maude was filling pretty glass bowls with cranberries and pickles that were made just for Christmas dinner. The house was full, and Elizabeth was happy. She looked down at the ring on her finger, which she still wore. Heman would be happy too.

The men were in the den. Alexander was passing out shots of whiskey to John Winslow and Eric Rood, his brothers-in-law, and Ed, Kate's father. Alexander had fond memories of his father, Heman, serving "Irish Coffee." Christmas was always a magical time.

"Where's Wayne?" Eric could not help noticing he was missing.

"He insisted he could take care of the horses by himself," Alexander answered.

"Your horses will be well taken care of." Ed knew how well Wayne did his job.

"Tell you the truth, I believe he wanted to play in the snow with the children. The snow is just right for a good snowball fight." Alexander took a seat close to the Christmas tree.

"How's the store, John?" Eric started a conversation that lasted until the ladies would call them to the dining room. That was two hours later.

Kate was given the job of bringing everyone to the dining room. "Dinner is served, gentlemen," she announced, as she stood in the doorway of the den.

"Music to my ears." John was the first one out of his chair.

"Bring your chairs," Kate added as she turned towards the staircase. "Everyone upstairs, it's time to eat. Children, can you hear me?" She could hear many footsteps heading for the landing on the second floor. "Be careful, don't fall down those stairs."

Kate turned just as her father was the last to leave the den. "Father, where is Edward?" This was the first time she had a free moment to ask. She also noticed that her sister, Maude, was carrying a peace sign in everything she said and did.

"Sweet Kate, of course, it would be you who noticed Edward's absence." Ed gave his youngest daughter a hug. "We don't know, Kate. He came back from Truro, and we had a wonderful few days. Better than we've had in years. Then he was gone. Just gone. Your mother is sick about it. We just don't know, Kate."

"We'll talk later." Kate wasn't going to break the peace between her and her sister. There would be other times; today she would hold her tongue. However, she couldn't help wondering about her brother, Edward.

The men headed for the dining room. The children followed Kate's instructions and headed for the kitchen. They had a table set just for them. There were ten places set in the dining room and seven in the kitchen. Lloyd was the leader amongst all the cousins in the kitchen. There did not seem to be a leader in the dining room.

It got very quiet as everyone looked at what was set before them. The best dishes, the red serviettes, and every serving bowl in the house were filled with food. It smelled heavenly.

Alexander turned to his mother, Elizabeth. "Would you like to say something, Mother?"

"Yes." Elizabeth slowly brought her feeble body to a standing position.

"You children, be quiet in the kitchen, your grandmother has something to say." Alexander turned back to his mother. "It's okay, Mother, we can hear you now."

"Thank you, dear." Elizabeth's eyes were misty as she spoke. "Merry Christmas and a Happy New Year to you all. May the year 1914 be full of joy, full of love, and our plates never be empty. I love you all, and Heman your father would have been proud of everyone who is in our home today. Now let us eat before this wonderful food gets cold."

"Hear, hear, God bless us all." Alexander started passing bowls around the table. The sounds of family love could be heard as they enjoyed this very special Christmas.

*****

"Happy New Year!" Rosemary lifted her glass of punch. "Happy New Year, Edward!" She took his hand into hers.

"I'm so glad you're here. I'm glad you came back from Sheet Harbour."

Edward was glad he came back from Sheet Harbour too. He was starting a new life. He would never go back to Sheet Harbour again. He smiled at Rosemary. "To you, my dear, may this be a year to remember." He didn't know why, but he felt better than he had ever felt. He walked with a lighter step, and he actually saw things around him. The rolling hills of Truro were calling to him. He was home now.

"Father said you could go back to work with him." Rosemary was happy her father was not upset with Edward. "You know he says you're as strong as an ox and has missed you working for him."

"You can tell your father I'll be back to work the first of the week."

"You can tell me yourself." Rosemary's father pulled up a chair and joined the two at their table.

"Yes, I can. Nice to see you again." Edward was growing closer to this man every time he saw him.

"You back to stay?"

"Yes, I am. Truro is now my home." Edward was surprised he could say that so easily.

213

"Well, great," he winked at Rosemary. "I'll leave you to your celebrating. See you the first of the week." He was rising from his chair as he spoke and took it with him as he walked away.

Chapter Eleven

Look for My Brother

C an I help you?"

"My brother is missing."

Patrick had been working as a clerk for the Halifax Police Department for two years now. Being an Irish immigrant himself, he took notice of others who weren't native to these parts. The man standing in front of his desk was certainly not from around here. Patrick was sure of that. The man had only spoken four words, and Patrick knew where he was from – Syria, and he was most likely a peddler. Patrick knew how hard it was for a man like this to find a job, for it was even hard for him. However, being from Syria, it was worse.

A cluster of Syrians lived together close to this police station; others lived closer to the docks. A close-knit people, they took care of each other. Patrick was actually surprised to see this man standing before him. They usually took care of their own problems.

"Your brother is missing?"

"Yes, my brother, Charles Asaff, is missing."

"Missing from where?"

"He's a peddler but hasn't come home. He was expected home a month ago. His wife and children haven't seen him. He always comes home"

"Wait a minute. Are you sure he's missing? Maybe he just ran away with a beautiful woman. You know it has been known to happen."

"No, sir, not my brother, not Charles. He loves his wife and babies. Something is very wrong. He is missing. I need help to find him."

Patrick looked into this man's eyes and he saw fear. "What is your name?"

"Joseph Asaff."

It must have taken a lot of courage for this man to come to the police department this morning, Patrick was thinking.

"Sit over there, Mr. Asaff. I will see if I can get a sergeant to talk to you. Can't promise you anything." Their eyes met for a second, and then Joseph Asaff shuffled over to a wooden chair and slowly sat in it. He turned his grey cap repeatedly in his lap, as he looked straight down at the floor.

Patrick knocked at the captain's door. He opened it when he heard, "Come on in."

"What can I do for you, Patrick?" The captain liked Patrick, even though he was from Ireland. He was a good man, and things seemed to work more smoothly since he took over out front a couple years ago.

"Captain, there's a bloke out here." Patrick looked towards the front office. "He says his brother is missing."

"Missing from where?"

"That's what I asked, sir. He's a Syrian."

"A Syrian?"

"Yes, sir, his brother, a peddler, is missing. I thought, since it has been pretty quiet around here the last few days, someone could talk to him."

"How long has he been missing?"

"He says over a month."

"You're right, it's time Sergeant Northover does a little work for his keep. Go talk with him."

"Yes, sir." Patrick left the room, closing the door quietly behind him. He started down a short hallway lit only by a light bulb hanging from the ceiling. The light bulb caused the white walls to glow yellow, mixed with dark shadows. He stopped before two doors, one on the right, and one on the left. Patrick knocked on the door to the left and waited. When he didn't hear an answer, he knocked a second time. Finally, he was summoned to enter.

"Sergeant Northover, the captain has sent me to inform you there is a client out front."

Clarence Northover was busy pitching baseball cards into a basket on the other side of the room. "You don't say, Patrick," as he sailed another card across the room, missing the basket by inches. "What can you tell me about him?"

"His brother is missing?"

"How long?"

"More than a month."

Sergeant Northover placed the stack of baseball cards on his desk. "And?"

"He's a Syrian. His brother is a peddler who was supposed to be back home a month ago."

"I don't know, Patrick. I don't have time for this."

Patrick looked around the room and back to Sergeant Northover's desk, which was empty, except the baseball cards. "Looks like you have all the time in the world. The Syrian's name is Joseph Asaff. You can talk to him, and then report back to the captain."

"Well, I have been looking for a puzzle to work on. Maybe this will keep me busy for a while."

"Thanks, Sergeant. Mr. Asaff looks really worried, so take it easy on him."

*****

Sergeant Northover was sitting in the captain's office. It had only been an hour since he sent Joseph Asaff on his way, promising him he would look into the matter. "Captain, looks like we may have something here. Sounds like this Charles Asaff went missing when there is no cause for it. My opinion is someone should look into it." Northover flipped through the notes he had just taken. "This peddler's route was along the Eastern Shore. Been doing the same route for over a year now. He thought it was a good route, made money, liked the people, and the people seemed to like him. Always came home every other week for more supplies.

Very odd for him not to come back for more supplies. And it was just before Christmas. His wife has been waiting each day for his return. That was over a month ago. His brother and sister believe that something isn't right."

"How did he travel the Eastern Shore?"

"Boat and stagecoach. Stagecoach mainly."

"I don't see how I can spare you here, while you run off chasing rabbits. I know it is slow right now, but you know and I know that can change like the weather. We had better call in the Dominion Police."

The captain opened the office door. "Patrick, I need you in here." His voice was loud and carried down the short hallway. Patrick was there seconds after the request was made.

"Yes, sir."

"Get me the Dominion Police Station in Truro on the phone."

"Yes, sir." One of the best parts of Patrick's job was using the phone, especially the long distance calls. Just imagine talking to someone in Truro. Truro was over an hour away as the crow flies. He picked up the telephone set, placed the receiver to his ear with his right hand, and clicked the cradle with his left. Click, click. "Operator, operator."

"This is the operator speaking, what is your number please?"

"Hi, Sally, it's Patrick here. I need 707 Truro – Dominion Police Station."

"Hi, Patrick, having a good day?"

"Since I am talking to you, my day is going fine."

Sally laughed. "It will take me a minute to put that call through."

"Call me when it's ready." Patrick had hung up the receiver, but he was staring at the phone. *It won't take long,* he thought. He jumped when the phone rang. He always jumped when the phone rang. It was almost as if it came to life. Picking up the receiver, he spoke plainly, "Halifax Police Station, how may I help you?"

"Hi, Patrick, I have that call to Truro ready."

"Thanks, Sally, let me go get the captain."

"Is this Dominion Police Department?"

"Yes, sir."

"I need to talk to Captain Harry. Is he around?"

"Yes, sir. One moment please."

Just like the Halifax Police Department, there was one phone at the front desk. It didn't take long before there was a "hello" coming across the earpiece.

"Good day to you, Captain. I believe I have a case for you."

Captain Harry took notes, as the details of the case were given to him. "Thanks. I think that's all I need. How's the weather in Halifax? Foggy you say? No, the sun is shining here, but it is to turn cold this very evening and stay that way for some time. Thanks again. I'll keep you informed. Goodbye." Captain Harry organized his notes in front of him. A Charles Asaff, a peddler is missing. His trade route was Eastern Shore. *I think I need to hire a detective.* He was talking to himself.

"Tom." The clerk, hearing his name, turned towards Captain Harry. "Get me a detective, Tom. Have him in my office this afternoon."

*****

It was not the first time Detective Walter Shanks was summoned to the Dominion Police Department. Shanks had a detective agency, and he had an office right on Main Street. Mind you, there were only the two of them, but they seemed to keep busy enough. The government always called upon them for the Dominion Police Department, and the government always paid on time. Shanks was whistling a tune as he entered the police station.

Captain Harry leaned over the desk and shook Shanks' hand. "How's business?" Captain Harry tightened his grip.

Shanks liked a firm handshake; it could tell the inside of a man. He had known Captain Harry for years now and knew he was tough as nails. "Business has been a little quiet since the first of the year. All this snow, I guess the bad guys are staying close to their fireplaces."

The Captain chuckled as he offered Shanks a seat in front of his desk. "I believe I have a job for you."

After all the details were spoken to Shanks, there was a time of silence, where he was trying to take it all in.

"So, where will you begin?" the captain asked Shanks.

"Sheet Harbour, I will ride over there through Musquodoboit Valley and see what I can find out. Then I will backtrack his route to Ship Harbour. You know the other small coastal community on the peddler's route."

"Don't forget to keep a tally of your expenses."

"I won't. See you in a couple of weeks."

*****

A fortnight later, Shanks was leading his horse towards the entrance of Conrod House Hotel. He was very happy to see a hotel in Sheet Harbour. He had spent a very uncomfortable night in Middle Musquodoboit. There was no hotel, but he managed to get a bed at the shopkeeper's home. The problem was a baby cried all night long. He was sure he just had gotten to sleep when the rooster crowed and the morning had begun. He was thankful for the biscuits that were given to him as he continued his journey. However, when he attempted to share them with his horse, not even his horse would eat them. Shanks was tired, hungry, and happy there was a hotel. He walked up to the desk and met a little old lady, with wrinkles on her face that matched her silver hair.

She looked up; for Shanks wasn't sure she even heard the bell ringing as he opened the door. A big smile smoothed out her wrinkles, "How do you do? Welcome! You're a stranger in these parts. You just passing through? Are you hungry? I have the best food in Sheet Harbour."

"Yes, to all of the above." Shanks couldn't help smiling at this elderly lady. He had just witnessed a whole conversation spoken by one person – herself. "My horse is out front. I need to take care of him. Since he is my partner, only the best will do."

"Of course, Mr.. .?"

"Mr. Shanks. Walter Shanks."

"Well, Mr. Walter Shanks, only the best for your partner.

"Frank!" Mrs. Conrod turned her head for a moment. A man almost as old as she came out of a back room. "Frank, this is Mr. Shanks. His horse needs tending, only the best for his partner."

Frank tipped his head in an acknowledgment and went through the front door. He disappeared, as the door closed behind him, leaving the sound of a bell ringing.

"Now, let's take care of you, Mr. Shanks. Would you like to eat, or would you need a room to refresh yourself before supper?"

"A room would do nicely. A view of the harbour would be appreciated."

"The harbour is frozen over, but tomorrow you can see ice skaters and a few people trying their luck at ice fishing. Trying to put food on their table, they are. I believe I have just what you have in mind. Where are you from? Or should I even ask such a question?" Mrs. Conrod handed him the book to sign his name.

Shanks again smiled at this lady. She reminded him of his own grandmother. He believed he was going to like staying at her hotel. "Truro, I'm from Truro. Came through Musquodoboit Valley."

"Oh, dear, that must have been a cold journey. Not many people make that trip this time of the year. Luckily, you were not stuck in a snowstorm. It can be dangerous out there this time of the year."

"You're correct that no one travels this time of the year. Mighty pretty, though. The snow hanging on the fir trees and covering the farmland. The last day of my journey, I only had my horse to talk to. I'm looking forward to having a conversation with someone who can answer me back. Mrs. Conrod, would you and Frank join me for supper? Maybe you could help me get to know these parts."

Mrs. Conrod was delighted to be invited.

*****

Mrs. Conrod had a special table prepared for her new guest, Water Shanks. She even placed a centrepiece in the middle. She would have placed real flowers there, but where was one to find real flowers in January?

As she was arranging the table, the bell of the front door sounded as John McPhee came through it. Snow covered his hat, shoulders, and feet. "It's cold enough to freeze. . . ."

"Don't you move, John MacPhee! Wait right there. For pity's sake, don't walk snow through the whole place." Mrs. Conrod could speak to John in this manner, for they had known each other for years. In fact, she watched him grow up. "I didn't even know it was snowing." She was spreading newspapers on the floor in front of John.

"Yes, it started just after sunset. What's for supper?"

John was a regular here at the Conrod House Hotel. He didn't have anyone to cook for him, and Mrs. Conrod cooked a whole lot better than he did. "Salt pork with creamy gravy. Hang your coat over there. For pity's sake, take those boots off."

John looked down at his boots. Pools of water were getting larger at his feet. "I guess I can. I just happen to have my best-knitted socks on. Thanks to you, a very nice Christmas present, they were too. That salt pork and creamy gravy sound good to my rumbling stomach. I just love the way you name your food. The sound of creamy gravy makes it taste even better."

"You'll have to sit over there, John. I can't join you for supper."

John spied the table set as pretty as a picture, just like in those fancy city magazines. "You got company, you have?"

"Yes, a Mr. Walter Shanks from Truro. He made that trip through Musquodoboit Valley. Just him and his horse."

"He got here just in time. I wouldn't want to make that trip in the snow."

"That's what I told him."

"What's he doing here? Must be important business to make that trip. How long is he staying?"

"I don't know, John. Frank and I are having supper with him. He should be down shortly. Now you just sit over there and mind your business. You hear me?" Mrs. Conrod didn't wait for an answer. She went back into the kitchen to make sure everything was just right.

By the time Detective Shanks entered the dining room, most of the tables were filled. Joe and Mariea Malay put down their knife and fork to watch the stranger walk through the dining room. At the table in the middle of the room sat Doug Chittick and Jerusha Balcom. They stopped their talking to take in this stranger from Truro. John had already spread the word.

Dr. Finlay MacMillan was sitting by himself at a corner table. He was the only one who didn't stop eating. He didn't have time, for he was just informed a baby was to be born that very night. He hated the thought of going out in that snow. Nevertheless, he would do what he always did. First, baby or no baby, he was going to eat his supper.

"Welcome, welcome." Mrs. Conrod entered the dining room. "Mr. Shanks, come this way and sit at this table. Frank is on his way. He says your horse is warm and comfortable in the horse shed. Nasty weather out there, it's a good thing you were not traveling tonight."

"Yes, I agree. This room, the warmth of your fireplace, and your company will make it an enjoyable evening." Detective Shanks enjoyed eating the salt pork with the creamy gravy over their boiled potatoes, and the rolls were the best he had ever tasted. The gooseberry jam, which he had never tasted, added a sweet taste to those soft rolls.

Detective Shanks' stomach was now full and he was a happy man. He was ready for conversation with his new friends. Folding his napkin and placing it beside his empty plate, he said, "Now more conversation would add to this wonderful supper."

"A little conversation before desert would be delightful." Mrs. Conrod had watched this man eat his whole dinner in silence, which she thought was very odd. She wanted to know more about him.

After the getting to know you talk, Shanks just came out with his mission. "I'm looking for someone. Maybe you can help."

"We know everyone around here, especially her." Frank gestured to Mrs. Conrod. "I'm sure we can be of help."

Maybe I will be lucky tonight, thought Shanks. "Do you know of a Charles Asaff?"

"We certainly do! He's our peddler from Halifax. We and everyone in Sheet Harbour are very fond of him."

"He can play the best music on his oud."

"Oud you say?"

Frank was quick to answer, "Oud is sort of like a banjo, but it has deeper sounds."

"Whenever he enters a room, a party breaks out. Everybody loves his music," Mrs. Conrod replied.

"When did you seen him last?"

"Well, that's funny you asked, isn't it Frank? Because we were just talking about that the other day. It was way before Christmas. He left a bag behind. I have it waiting for him at the front desk. We usually see him before now. However, the weather has been cruel. He usually stays here."

"Why do you want to find Asaff?" Mrs. Conrod just realized it was odd that this stranger was asking about the peddler.

"When was the last time you saw him? It's very important that I know every detail."

Frank turned to Mrs. Conrod. "Do you remember, dear?"

"Yes, I remember very well. He and several men from the ship were eating dinner right over there at that table. He was happy, for he had finished his trade route early. He was going back to Halifax on the stagecoach the next day. He was going to stay there and be with his family until after Christmas. Come to think of it, he didn't even say goodbye."

"Did he usually say goodbye?"

"Why, yes, he pays his bill and says goodbye. But that day he paid before supper, and after supper, he left with someone."

"I remember," Frank interrupted. "He left with Edward Cook, didn't he?"

"Yes, he did." Mrs. Conrod was looking down at her plate.

"Who is Edward Cook?"

"The most meanest, baddest, rotten person in all of Sheet Harbour." That is what Frank thought of him.

"But he was different that night." Mrs. Conrod was still looking at her empty plate. "He had been away for awhile. Truro, he said he had been to Truro."

"Truro?" Shanks thought that was very interesting. "If this Cook was so mean, why did the peddler go somewhere with him?"

"The peddler didn't know Cook like the rest of us did."

Mrs. Conrod looked up from her plate. "I heard Edward tell the peddler, his parents needed things for a party. Edward asked the peddler to go with him. His folks are such nice people. They did everything for him. They tried their best. Why are you asking these questions? What is your business here in Sheet Harbour?"

I guess I cannot go any further without telling them, thought Shanks. "The peddler is missing. I'm a detective hired by the Dominion Police Department to find him."

The whole dining room fell silent. Not a fork or spoon could be heard touching plates and bowls, for every person in the room had been listening to the whole conversation taking place at Shanks' table.

"I believe the first place to start is Edward Cook. Where can I find him?"

"I haven't seen him around, which is a good thing for us." Frank turned to Mrs. Conrod. "Whenever he comes around here, there's trouble. We have a list of things we can tell you. The list is as long as your arm."

"But, Frank, he was different that night. When he came in here, you could even talk with him. He was just different somehow."

"Where does he live?"

"Cook Road."

Of course, Shanks thought. Edward Cook lives on Cook Road. Where else would an Edward Cook live? He made a note of this in his journal. "How do I get to this Cook Road?"

John MacPhee stood and walked over to where Shanks was sitting. "I know where he lives. I'll take you tomorrow."

Chapter Twelve

"Your Sins Will Find You Out"

Numbers 32:23

It's funny how one minute life is fine, and then . . .

Kate and Elizabeth were sitting at the kitchen table. Breakfast was over. The older children were off to school. Just above them, footsteps could be heard from the younger ones playing upstairs. Alexander and Wayne had taken the sleigh and headed towards the post office. It was the first trip that way for ten days. The weather had been fierce, for snow had fallen every other day. It seemed like all Alexander and Wayne did was shovel a pathway from the house to the barn. It even snowed through the night; they woke up to several more inches.

The sun was shining this morning. Elizabeth and Kate were thankful for the warmth of the kitchen. The cook stove did its job well performing double duty, both cooking the food and heating the home. The wood box by the back door was always full of fresh-split cured wood. They sipped on hot coffee, enjoying each other's company. For one thing about winter, they had more time to sit around and visit and just do family things.

It was just the calm before the storm. Kate would remember well how that quiet, lazy, winter morning turned upside down, changing her life forever.

They were not even finished sipping their coffee. They were thinking about clearing the table and washing dishes. Just the regular things that one did every morning. However, the dishes would not be washed that morning.

Elizabeth saw the sleigh come speeding into the laneway and Alexander jump out before they reached the well. She thought they must have forgotten something and knew not what. They were not gone long enough to go to the post office and back. It was very odd when Alexander came through the door and into the kitchen without even taking his boots off. Snow went everywhere. Elizabeth remembered his words very well.

"Kate, get your coat. There's something going on at your parents' house. I came back for you."

Of course, Kate wanted to ask what was going on, but she just sat there frozen.

"Come, Kate, there are police at your parents' house. Elbridge told us at the ferry when we arrived."

Elizabeth put down her coffee cup and told Kate to go. She would take care of the children.

Wayne was waiting in the sleigh as Alexander and Kate climbed inside. It wasn't long before the sleigh was back out on the snow-covered road. The horses wanted to run. They had been in the barn for ten days. Wayne, holding tightly to the reins, let them go. Kate held on for dear life. Alexander only knew something was terribly wrong, and they needed to go and find out what.

There were no signs of life as they passed Maude's store. Alexander had noticed it the first time they passed by. Elbridge told him Maude was already on the way to her parents' house.

Wayne didn't say a word; he was concentrating on keeping the horses going forward. Even though Kate was under an old buffalo coat, fear had caused her blood to run cold. There was silence between them, for there was nothing to say.

The sun was shining on the white drifted snow, throwing the light of millions of diamonds in every direction. The fir trees hung heavy with the snow that had fallen there. The tide was high in the harbour; one could hear the sound of the ice cracking as the water moved forward under the ice. Nevertheless, they did not notice any of this. For they had too many questions going around and around in their heads. Questions and no answers.

There was a line at the ferry. Two sleighs were ahead of them; however, when Elbridge saw them coming, he raised his hand in the air, directing them to the front of the line and first on the ferry. Both Wayne and Alexander jumped out of the sleigh. "Have you heard anything?"

"Only that all of Sheet Harbour is talking about it. I'm told a crowd is forming."

Alexander knew he was not telling everything. He was holding something back.

When another sleigh was aboard the ferry, they had four men to help pull the ropes to get to the other side. Even with gloves, their hands were wet and cold.

It seemed like time had stopped. What seemed like hours was only half the time, when they finally turned onto East River Road. Wayne was still allowing the horses to have their way. Kate just knew they were going too fast for the right turn that was just ahead of them. The sleigh slid on the fresh snow and came around half circle, and Kate hanging on for dear life, barely kept from screaming out, but the sleigh straightened itself and continued following the horses. Kate looked to see what was up ahead.

There were sleighs and horses off both sides of Cook Road. It looked as if there was a party. Wayne guided Beauty and Molly straight between all the traffic. They did not stop until they were in front of Kate's parents' house.

There were a dozen or more people waiting outside the door. They made an opening for Kate and Alexander to pass through. They did not knock; they opened the door and closed it quickly behind them. It was as if they entered another world. No one seemed to notice their arrival. Voices could be heard in the parlour.

"Here, Kate, let me take your coat." Alexander was already removing his own. Snow boots were added to a pile. Kate thought there were enough there to start a shoe store. She shook her head to clear her mind. What a thing to think of at a time like this. Maybe it was because she did not have a clue to what was happening.

Still, no one knew they were there. Footsteps could not be heard in stocking feet, as they walked down the hallway to the parlour. They were standing in the doorway before anyone noticed their presence.

It was only a few seconds, but Kate saw her parents sitting on the chesterfield, Maude standing behind them. There were four men in the room. One was John Winslow, and could that really be John McPhee? What was he doing here? There was Father and the other was a complete stranger. The stranger had his back towards Kate, and she could see he was doing most of the talking.

Kate's mind was running so fast that she took a sigh of relief. No one was dead, at least that she could see. All family members were accounted for, all except Edward. Kate's heart turned cold again.

"Kate, Alexander." Maude came forward towards them.

"What's happened, Maude? What's going on?"

"Oh, Kate." It was her mother. "They found that poor peddler."

The stranger stood and so did her father.

"Kate, this is Walter Shanks from Truro. You know John McPhee." He pointed to the other chair.

"Yes, of course." Alexander went to shake his hand.

Ed looked upon Shanks. "This is Kate our other daughter, her husband, Alexander."

"Please come in." Shanks was taking control.

Alexander could see there was nowhere else to sit. "I will get two chairs from the dining room."

When everyone was settled again, Ed and Flo sat on the chesterfield, Maude and John on a settee by the window, the two men on oversized stuffed chairs. These were the very chairs that her parents often sat in, her father reading the paper and her mother knitting. Kate shook her head again to clear her mind. Alexander and she stood out like sore thumbs, for they were sitting on dining room chairs that were placed right in the middle of the room.

Shanks began, "As I've already told your family, I'm a detective from Truro. I'm investigating a missing peddler, Charles Asaff."

"Oh, they found him, right over there." Flo's arm went in the direction of the window. She covered her mouth with a lace handkerchief and sobbed quietly.

"Over where?" Alexander could not help but ask. Kate was glad he did, for she was very confused.

Mr. Shanks looked towards Ed. "She will be fine. You can continue."

"Yes, Mrs. Cook is correct. We found the peddler, John McPhee and I that is, found him about 60 feet, give or take a foot, off the road. He's dead."

"Dead?!" Kate could not help herself. "Dead! You mean Charles Asaff, our peddler is dead?"

"I'm afraid so."

"Well, how did he die? Furthermore, how come he was dead over there?" Kate was not sure if what she had just asked made any sense at all.

"That's what we're trying to find out. When was the last time you saw him? The peddler I mean."

"He was at my house." Alexander stopped for a moment to think. "The first of December."

"Yes, that's right." Kate looked at Alexander. "We bought Christmas presents from him."

"When was the last time you saw Edward?"

"Edward?!" Kate almost stood up from her chair.

"Yes, your brother, Edward. When was the last time you saw him?"

"Well, he was supposed to come for Christmas. That's what you said." Maude looked directly at Kate. "But as usual, he didn't show up."

"But we had a real nice visit." Kate was quick to add. "He came sometime in December. He was changed, he seemed happy. He was not as troubled."

"That's what I just finished telling the detective." Flo had stopped crying. "He had changed. He sat down and talked to both of us, didn't he Ed?"

"Yes, he had meals with us," Ed responded.

"That does not sound like the Edward I know." It was Maude. "Edward was always trouble. I didn't allow him in our house, isn't that right, John?"

"Where is Edward now?" Shanks was listening closely to what was being said.

"We don't know for sure. He didn't even say goodbye; however, my guess would be Truro. He talked a lot about Truro. But it was very strange he didn't say goodbye and just went off like that. Did he say goodbye to you girls?"

"No, Papa, he didn't."

Maude shook her head. "I never even saw him."

"Do you have a gun?"

"A gun? Was he shot?" Kate was almost out of her chair again.

"Yes, the peddler died of a gunshot wound to the back of the head."

"He would never have known it was coming." John McPhee spoke for the first time.

"Do you have a gun?" Shanks asked again.

"Yes, a handgun. I keep it in my desk." Ed had a sick feeling in his stomach. When he retrieved it, he gave it to the detective.

*****

Shanks was back in his office. He had spent four days in Sheet Harbour. The unpleasant job of sending the peddler's body back to Halifax was done. Because of winter, he had to arrange for a Packet boat to deliver it to Halifax Harbour. There the police would meet it and have a coroner look at the body to document all they needed for a trial. Afterward, they would deliver the body to Charles Asaff's family. After talking with several more people around Sheet Harbour, Shanks headed back through the Middle Musquodoboit Valley to Truro.

Shanks had just spent more than an hour talking to Captain Harry at the police station, going over all the notes he had taken about the case. They had a murder on their hands. Now to find out who did it. Their number one suspect was Edward Cook. They did have another suspect, a Keith Seaford. He lived several miles away from Sheet Harbour. There was no evidence of him ever being up on Cook Road.

They would start with Edward Cook. He was right on their doorstep. However, before Shanks even tried to find him in Truro, a big lead in the case fell right into their laps. A telephone call came into the Truro Police Station. It was from Alfred Dudley Brown, the Postmaster from the Main Post Office in Truro. Mr. Brown was passing on information that he thought questionable. A gentleman was at the post office trying to cash a post office order for the amount of $15.00. The man didn't have any identification to prove he was the man named on the cheque. He got really nervous and left. The name on the cheque was a Mr. Charles Asaff.

******

Edward was eating lunch. He was with a group of men who worked together in the rail yard. Life was good for Edward; he had a job, he had a girl, and he felt a part of this group. Edward could talk with them and they could talk to him. It didn't matter what they talked about; it was just the passing of the day talk.

Edward was just closing the lid of his lunch box when Rosemary's father came around the corner and into the shack where the men ate their lunches. It was not a very large shack, but it kept the men out of the cold. All the men looked towards the boss, for it was unusual indeed to see the boss at lunchtime. He greeted the men and then turned to Edward.

"A Walter Shanks is in my office. He wants to talk with you. Do you know him?"

"No, I don't believe I've ever heard that name before."

"Come with me, we'll see what he wants." As they walked along, he spoke to Edward about how he enjoyed the past Sunday dinner at his house. "Rosemary has taken a liking to you." He winked at Edward as they entered the office.

He turned to Walter Shanks sitting on this side of his desk. "This is Edward Cook."

"Edward Cook, I need to take you down to the police station. We have some questions to ask you."

"What is this about, is Edward in some kind of trouble? Are you a police officer?"

"No, sir, but I need for Edward to come with me."

Edward had no idea why this man would want to ask him questions. He never saw this man before. "If it's okay with you, boss, I'll go with him, and then I'll tell you all about it when I get back."

However, Edward never went back to the lunchroom. He never again talked to Rosemary or her father.

Edward was in a room with both Walter Shanks and Captain Harry. He wouldn't answer the question, "Do you have a post office order for the amount of $15.00 made out to a Charles Asaff?"

Edward didn't even panic. He brought the cheque out of his wallet. "This cheque?" He offered it to Shanks.

Shanks took the cheque and looked it over. "Where did you get it?"

"The peddler gave it to me."

"Why did the peddler give it to you?"

Edward began to sweat just a little. The peddler's face flashed before him. A face with a bullet hole in the back of his head. He tried to clear his mind, but his mind was talking to him. *It was all the peddler's fault. He got me all riled up when he said he was at Sober Island. Nothing good comes from Sober Island.*

"Why did the peddler give it to you?" Shanks asked again.

"I did work for him. I sold him a wagon."

"Why did the peddler not write this cheque over to you? I don't see anywhere on this cheque where it says your name." Shanks was turning the cheque repeatedly in his hands. "That must have been some wagon. A fifteen dollar wagon? And why would a peddler want a wagon?"

Edward began to sweat.

"Are you hot, Edward?"

"Yes, the temperature is warm in this room."

Shanks went over and touched the three-legged potbelly stove. It had not been used in two days. In fact, it was cold in the room.

"Edward, I don't need to ask any more questions."

This is when Captain Harry took over. "Edward Cook, I arrest you for the murder of Charles Asaff. You have the right to retain and instruct counsel without delay. Do you understand? Do you wish to call a lawyer? Do you understand?"

Edward placed his face in his hands. Then softly they could hear his reply, "I understand."

Chapter Thirteen

The View from the Window

T hey can't do it! Why should they do it?!" Maude was livid she was so mad. "Mother and Papa are not taking a mortgage out on their house. The house is completely paid for and has been for many years. They don't owe a penny on it. They're old; they don't need this debt hanging over their heads."

"But you know they will." Kate was surprised how angry Maude was. "Edward is their son."

"That is not true and you know it, Kate!"

"I've said it before, Maude. . ."

"Yes, I know what you're going to say. He became family when Papa brought that baby into the house. But he has been nothing but trouble right from the beginning."

"Papa thinks of him as a son. He gave him his own name, Edward Junior. He'll never give up on him."

"Lawyers are very expensive, Kate."

"Papa knows that. He'll mortgage his house."

"What if Edward is guilty? What if he killed that peddler?"

"Papa and Mother don't think Edward did it. When he was home for that last visit, Edward had changed. Papa saw it, Mother saw it, and I saw it. He just couldn't have killed the peddler. Why would he kill the peddler, Maude?"

"The trial will be coming up. Where is the lawyer going to find one person in Sheet Harbour who would say Edward was a good person? One person, Kate? Yes, maybe Papa, Mother, and you. But who else? In fact, I hear they're lining up to tell how mean he was. Plus, they all have a story to tell. John McPhee, Joe and Mariea Malay, Doug Chittick, and Jerusha Balcom, all have horror stories of Edward causing trouble at the Conrod Hotel. That's just the beginning. Roy Kenney says Edward tried to kill him twice. Once when he shared a room with Edward at the hotel. He tried to smother him with a pillow when he slept. Then another time Edward was on the veranda of the hotel where he had a gun. Shot at him five times. One bullet went right through the sun hat he was wearing at the time."

"Come now, Maude. Roy is what eight or nine years old? Seems to me he wants to get in on all the excitement, with everyone in Sheet Harbour talking about the peddler being killed. How are you going to believe what is true and what is not? And I don't like your attitude. Never have. I don't want to talk to you about this anymore."

"Well, Kate, having a store, people are coming in and they're talking. I'm telling you, Edward doesn't have a chance."

"I hope you're wrong, Maude."

*****

Officer Patrick started down the short hallway lit by the single light bulb. The same light bulb that caused the white walls to glow yellow mixed with dark shadows. However, his usual stop before the two doors, one on the right and one on the left had been altered recently. This time he continued farther down the hall to the very end. Here was a door facing him. He continued up a wooden staircase to the second floor. There on the landing, he faced yet another door. He needed a key to open this door. He had just the one on a brass ring connected to his belt. There were many keys on the ring; his finger found the one he was looking for.

He noticed his fingers were shaking just a little. It didn't surprise him, for he was quite apprehensive every time he unlocked this door and entered the room. Actually, it was bigger than just a room. This door led to a whole corridor, which was 25 to 30 feet in length and almost as wide. It was not dark and dreary like the downstairs hallway. There were windows all along one wall, providing plenty of light for the room and a beautiful view below. The harbour, that is. Blue water, bluer than the blue sky. Halifax Harbour, where ships entered and departed daily.

However, that didn't stop him from being apprehensive, for on the other side of this door is where they kept a murderer. Edward Cook had the whole place to himself. Patrick had no trouble with Edward. Still, it was a strange thing to keep a murderer up here.

Excitement filled the town the day Edward Cook came to the police station from Truro. It had been years since the police station had to deal with a murder case. They didn't even have a jail cell to put him in. The cells were all full. That was a lucky break for Cook since it was decided to keep him upstairs here. Just lock him in.

Patrick put the key in the lock and turned it. Opening the door, he immediately saw Cook. He was sitting at the table beside the window, writing something. Patrick gave a sigh of relief; he always feared in such a large space he would not be able to find him. On the other hand, Cook could be hiding just waiting for him.

Patrick walked over to the table. "Mr. Cook, I'm here to give you a message. A. . ." Patrick looked down at the paper he was carrying. "J. O'Hearn is coming to see you, sometime this afternoon."

"Who is O'Hearn?" Edward asked.

"A criminal lawyer."

"And who is paying for this criminal lawyer?"

"That question I cannot answer since I don't know. He's one of the best in the city. And he knows everybody worth knowing in and out of court around these parts."

Edward didn't seem to hear. Patrick was about to turn and leave when Edward's voice could be plainly heard. "Could I see a minister?"

"What did you say?" Patrick wanted to make sure he heard him right.

"Could I see a minister, a man of God?"

"I will ask the captain. Is that all?"

Edward didn't answer; he just looked out the window watching the world go by as he sat at the table.

*****

O'Hearn had gotten the case a week ago. A murder case in Halifax. Money for his retainer was coming from the suspect's parents. The money wouldn't go very far, but that didn't matter. O'Hearn would have taken the case for free. Not that the parents knew that. A murder case didn't come along very often. You had to be at the right place at the right time. That's where O'Hearn found himself, at the right place at the right time. He had already questioned the detective from Truro. Shanks, a Walter Shanks and Captain Harry from the Dominion Police Station in Truro. Shanks went with him to talk to Edward's boss. A Murphy, who had many men working under him at the railroad. They sat in his office. The first question Murphy asked was, "Where is Edward Cook, for I have not seen him in some time. He has just vanished." When he was told Edward was under arrest for the murder of a peddler, he almost turned his chair over. "Can't be," he replied. "He is seeing my daughter. He has been to my home. Surely, I would have seen something out of the ordinary."

O'Hearn took mental notes. Here is someone who can stand in the courtroom and give a good testimony for my client. "Your daughter, you say? How long was Edward seeing. . .?" He looked at Murphy. "Your daughter's name?

"Rosemary."

"Rosemary -- a pretty name. How long was Edward seeing Rosemary?"

"They met the beginning of summer. I had a community dance in my town, Bible Hill. I invited the men that work for me. Edward got to know my daughter that night. He has been in our home many times since. She has been worried sick, not hearing from Edward."

"Would you testify in his favour? Would Rosemary testify in his favour?"

"Yes, I would, and I am sure Rosemary would also."

*****

O'Hearn thought he had a very productive day. Now he would have to go to Sheet Harbour to see what he could find out there.

Sheet Harbour wasn't anything like Truro. O'Hearn couldn't find anyone who had anything good to say about Edward. That is except his parents, a sister, and an old lady that ran a hotel. A Ms. Conrod, who kept saying Edward had changed; he was different the last time she saw him.

When O'Hearn got back to his office in Halifax, he was surprised to see a large envelope on his desk. It was from the prosecutor's office. Opening it, he saw a list of names, a mile long. It seemed everyone in Sheet Harbour was willing to go to court to tell how bad Edward was.

*****

"Do you know any of these people?" O'Hearn placed a list in front of Edward.

Louis Asaff	Theodore Martin (constable)	Jerusha Hall
Joseph Malay	Foster Farnell	Frances Hall
Maria Malay	Clyde Rutherford	Isaac Kenney
John Angus MacPhee	Rogers R. Robertson	Douglas Chittick
Roy B. Henley	Henry Hall	Thomas Hall
Robert Hall	Rogers Fisher	Dr. Kirk Maclellan
Fannie Sutherland	Dr. William D. Finn	Robert Harmon (a rifle expert)
John E. Murphy	G. Ross Marshall	Clarence Hall
F.W. Christie PLS	Susie Wright	Frank Hanrahan (a detective)
Daniel MacPherson	Perry Lindsay	Constable Fred Umlah
Patrick Coady	Irvin Whitman	Sadie Asaff
Dr. Finlay MacMillan	Edward S. White	Joseph Asaff

v

After Edward read all the names, he handed the paper back to O'Hearn. "I know most of them. Just a few names I don't know. Most of them I spent my whole life with in Sheet Harbour."

"All of these people are going to be at the trial. What do you think they will say?"

Before Edward could answer, O'Hearn continued, "Through all my days of being a lawyer, I've never seen a list of people this long that the Crown will present to the jury. What do they have to say, Edward?"

"That I'm a wild, mean, and ruthless man. I fought with anyone who would fight with me. And I won."

"If you acted like a wild, mean, and ruthless man, Edward, they would not allow you to be kept in this room." O'Hearn flung his arm around the room. "This is not a jail cell. You don't look like a wild, mean, and ruthless man to me."

"That is because I've changed. Rosemary Murphy – she changed me. Wasn't soon enough, was it?"

"Yes, we have been to Bible Hill, we talked. . . "

"You did what!" Edward was on his feet and his face was changing colour. "You did what? You have been to Bible Hill. Who said you could do that?" His face was a deep shade of red, and the veins in his neck were swelled and ready to break.

"Calm down." O'Hearn was also on his feet. "Calm down and sit back down in your seat. You must control yourself. You can't act like this, especially in court."

"Yes, both Terrell and I have been to Bible Hill. We are your defense lawyers. We have to find someone to stand in court and tell the judge they like you. Both Rosemary and her father, Mr. Murphy, plan to be here. They like you very much, and they can't see how you could do such a thing. Murder that is."

Edward was sitting in his chair. But he bowed forward with his head in his hands crying, "No, No, No. I will not have them here. Nowhere near here. No, it's too late. One, two, or even three people to say I'm not the person they described isn't enough. I don't want her anywhere near here. Nor her father. It's just too late." He looked up at O'Hearn, "Don't you understand? I don't want them to hear the stories that will be told about me. It's the same thing when I wouldn't see my father when he came all the way from Sheet Harbour. I don't want Rosemary and her father even in Halifax. Therefore, you will have to defend me without Rosemary, without her father, and without my mother and father. Do you get it?" Edward was back on his feet looking into the eyes of O'Hearn. "Do you get it?"

What was O'Hearn to say or do? He answered, "I get it."

*****

Patrick never saw so much foot traffic coming and going from the police station. The phone never stopped ringing. He was going to wear a pathway on the hardwood floor between the front of the station to the captain's office. He couldn't help overhearing the captain talking with Sergeant Northover. They had never seen so many big shot lawyers descend upon the station. The captain wasn't sure they even knew where the police station was until now. Everybody who was anybody wanted a piece of this murder trial.

The captain said, "The Prosecutor's office was like a circus. Everyone wanted to be assigned to this case; however, Deputy Attorney General, Stewart Jenks and A.G. Morrison, the Crown Prosecutor for Halifax County and his assistant, Andrew Cluney, will do it themselves. It will add a few feathers to their caps. I'm not surprised to hear that Walter O'Hearn, a criminal lawyer, was assigned to defend Cook at the trial because he is the best lawyer in town. O'Hearn, noticed how strong the prosecutor's team was, so he asked another lawyer, James Terrell[vi], to help, both being paid by Edward's parents. To top the list, the Justice, James J. Ritchie, will be the sitting judge. He called for a Supreme

Court jury. Guess who's on the jury." Before Northover could even guess, the captain answered, "John O'Neil, the world famous oarsman, he was nominated foreman of the jury. And guess who else. James O'Connor of the A. O'Connor Company. And Ralph Isnor of the new motorcar dealership downtown. These are just a few of the well-known citizens of Halifax assigned to the jury."

Northover summed it up, "This is big stuff." He shook his head.

"You can say that again." The captain walked down the hallway to his office. Before entering his office, he turned his head back down the hall towards Patrick. "Patrick, a minister will stop by to see Cook in the morning."

"Aye, aye, sir."

With that, the captain closed his door.

*****

Reverend Rogers pulled out a chair and sat down at the table. Edward was already sitting across the table from him. "Thanks for coming." There was a silence between them. "I don't know why I'm interested in God now," Edward began. "He never was with me when I was growing up in Sheet Harbour. That's when I needed Him. Now that I've changed,

I don't know what else to call it. I have a need to know more about Him. That is God, I mean."

Rogers loosened the white collar around his neck. That is how he could tell he was nervous. The collar always seemed tighter. He had never counseled a murderer before. He had not even met one until now. A murderer was sitting on the other side of the table from him. He didn't look like a murderer. He was a big man, but didn't look any different than those blokes that worked on the docks. *Maybe they got the wrong man. Just maybe he is innocent.*

All these thoughts were going around and around in his mind, like a waterspout he once saw going up the Bay of Fundy. He quickly brought his thoughts back to the present. Pulling his collar with two fingers, he brought himself to attention. "I'm here to answer your questions. That is, I will try. I may not know the answers, but I'm willing to hear the questions." Rogers thought that sounded good, even if he did say so himself. "Yes, I am here to answer any question you have." His fingers were no longer pulling at his collar. "Tell me about yourself?"

"There isn't much to tell. I grew up in Sheet Harbour. I was a troublemaker. A wild, mean, and ruthless man. As I look back, I don't even know why I acted that way. It's funny you know. I'm going to have to listen to all those people from Sheet Harbour tell their stories at the trial. However, they don't even know who I really am. I made up everything. Like a game and I held all the rules. I'm not the same person in their stories. I've changed. I have a peace of mind. Does that sound strange to you, Reverend?"

"No, not strange at all. I never knew you when you were known as the wild, mean, and ruthless man. Looking at you right now, sitting at this table, you are calm and seem to be in your right mind. It's obvious to me that you have changed. I'm sure God knows it. He knows these things before anyone else does. I'm far more interested in knowing you now."

Edward lifted his head and looked right into Reverend Rogers' eyes. "I've changed, but it's way too late for me. Satan had me all those years. He let me go after he was finished with me, after doing evil all around me. Like I said, it's too late for me. However, maybe someone can learn from me. Never let the devil rule your heart."

Reverend Rogers saw Edward often. He came most days, for Edward didn't have other visitors. One afternoon, Rogers brought a Crokinole board with him. They spent many hours playing that and a card game called 45s. It helped pass the time for Edward. He had never had a friendship with an older man before. He looked forward to every visit. They not only played games, they talked about God, His Son Jesus, and His love for him. *How could anyone love me?* he thought. But the Reverend said Jesus died on the cross for his sins. Jesus rose again from the grave three days later. All because He loved sinners. Sinners like him. Once, after Reverend Rogers had left, Edward sat at the table beside the window for an hour, contemplating on how people could learn something from the terrible thing he had done. He took his pencil and began to write:

Come all my Sheet Harbour friends,

With a broken down cast look,

Pay strict attention to these lines

Presented by Edward Cook.

Edward looked towards the harbour. He could see the ferry crossing the harbour heading towards Dartmouth. He looked down at his paper and his pencil moved again.

It was early last December,

I sealed my helpless doom,

To rob and kill a helpless man

Who strayed from his far home

I asked him to come with me

Down by the meadow gate

But little did poor 'Charlie' think

His precious life I'd take.

I put a bullet through his brain

Without the least regard.

The heavy swing of a sharp keen axe

He died an unknown death.

Edward lifted his head. He heard the sound of the key in the lock. The door would open. He quickly closed his notebook and placed his pencil on top. He glanced out the window. The ferry was returning to the wharf in Halifax. Later, I will finish this later.

Chapter Fourteen

Whoopee! I Made the List

You would think, after finding the peddler's body up on Cook Road two months ago, that things would have quieted down in Sheet Harbour. However, it had not. It was all anyone could talk about.

Winter was almost over, but not quite. It had been a wet March, and the road to Halifax was still impassable for the stagecoach. The mail was still coming by coaster boat. *The Marlis,* affectionately named by the residents of towns Marlie Joseph visited, was one of the regular mail carriers. During the winter, Marlie visited every small community along the Eastern Shore. Word passed quickly when *The Marlis* was seen coming into the Harbour. A crowd would gather at Bob Hall's house. It gave Bob, the postmaster, a short temper. He wanted everyone outside so he could sort the mail. Most days it was the Halifax newspapers that folks were looking for. They searched for any information about the murder case.

Today the mailbag seemed heavier to Bob. He opened it and discovered the reason for the extra weight. The bag contained several official looking letters in long, white envelopes, all were identically stamped: The Government of Halifax County.

The crowd outside seemed to be getting larger. John McPhee banged on the door, and to his amazement, the door opened, if only a little. He stuck his head through and, seeing Bob working at a table, he asked in sort of a loud voice, "Are you done yet? The crowd is getting very restless out here, they are."

"John McPhee, you get your head out of my door and close it. Do you hear? I will open that door when I am good and ready."

John closed the door, and turning to the group that had gathered, yelled, "There is something going on in there. He doesn't usually take this long."

John was the first one in and the first to see his letter. Tearing it open, his eyes went over the typed page. "Whoopee!" he exclaimed, "I made the list."

"What list?" Bob was the closest to him.

"I'm going to the trial! I'm going to a murder trial! Not only that, I'm going to testify. Boy, do I have a story to tell. That Edward will get what's coming to him, he will." John ran for the door. He was in a hurry to tell anyone in Sheet Harbour who would listen.

There were thirty-one government envelopes in all. Thirty-one people from Sheet Harbour would be going to the trial in Halifax to testify. They all had a different story to tell. And tell it, they would. They would all testify against Edward Cook. They were happy to do it. The way they acted you would think they just won the grand prize pig at the fair.

*****

Alexander was very careful when he went to pick up the mail. He made sure he was there just before closing. He did not want to walk through a crowd of people who wanted to hang his brother-in-law. Bob Hall had his mail waiting, and being a good friend of Alexander, he would keep him up to date on what was happening in Sheet Harbour.

Alexander and Kate stayed most of the time in Watt Section. Anytime they ventured into the Harbour, people would stare, point fingers, and talk behind their backs. You would think they had killed the peddler.

Kate was suffering terribly. She didn't sleep well. Alexander would find her sitting on a large rock beside the lighthouse, staring out at the ocean. She spent way too much time there alone. As usual, Alexander walked the pathway to the lighthouse. Even though it was the end of March, there were still patches of snow in the field, for it had been a long, cold winter. The wind coming off shore was cold. Alexander turned his collar up to protect his neck, for he was not wearing a scarf. From a distance, he could see the outline of his wife. She completed him. He could feel her hurt. He did not know how to protect her, which gave him grief indeed. How could she be protected from a murder case, especially if the one accused of committing the deed was her brother?

Kate turned to watch her husband coming towards her. The seagulls seemed to tell her he was coming. Alexander tried his best to console her, but her heart hurt so badly she was sure it was turning to ice.

"Kate, are you cold? I worry you will make yourself sick. It's too cold to sit here like you do."

"I'm fine, dear. See, I even have mittens to keep my hands warm. I sit here, and as I look out upon the ocean, I know what Mother Elizabeth means when she tells how the sea called your father, Heman. 'The calling of the sea,' she says. Yes, the sea seems to be calling. It would be so different out there. No more worry about Edward, no more worry about the trial, no more worries."

"Yes, but you would have to worry that a shark wouldn't get you. In addition, you would have to worry about the North Easter that could come upon you at any time. Believe me, I know; I have been there. Therefore, the sea does not call me. May my father rest in peace. He so wanted me to become the captain of his precious *Lady Catherine*. I couldn't do it."

Kate looked towards him and took his hand in hers. "I like you just the way you are." Kate broke the spell and let go of his hand. "Have you been to the post office?"

"Yes, and the news isn't good."

"How can it get worse, Alexander? Did you know Papa went to Halifax?" "Mother sent cookies and Edward's favourite raisin bread. Then they wouldn't let Papa see him. They took the food, but Papa went all the way to Halifax, and they wouldn't let him see his own son."

"Yes, I know. Keep that to yourself. All of Sheet Harbour has too much to talk about already."

"I'm sorry, I already told Maude."

"All of Sheet Harbour will know now."

Alexander changed the subject. "Do you know Isaac Kenney?"

"No, I don't think so?"

"Well, I do. He is part of the Kenneys on John Winslow's side. I just found out he will attend the trial."

"The trial? We don't even know there is going to be a trial. The Grand Jury was to determine if there was enough evidence for trial. I just know there wasn't enough evidence."

"I'm afraid they disagree with you. There will be a trial, and Isaac Kenney will testify against Edward. Not just him, but thirty other people from here in Sheet Harbour."

"That's awful. Maude was right. She said they would line up to do so. But thirty-one, that's awful. How do you know this?"

"Bob Hall, the postmaster, told me thirty-one people received letters from the government of Halifax this very day."

"My poor parents."

"Why don't you have them come and stay with us? We may be far enough away from all the hubbub."

"When?"

"Tomorrow morning. I will have Wayne hitch up Molly to the wagon. We will visit them and see how they are doing."

*****

Kate woke up to a beautiful sunny morning. Good weather to make the short trip to Cook Road. Kate was surprised she was looking forward to going. She awoke early and was ready before Wayne had the wagon ready to go. She hadn't left Watt Section in over a month. Hopefully, she could talk her parents into coming.

Kate didn't notice anything unusual on their journey, until they reached the ferry. There were two wagons ahead of them. Everyone became very quiet, while they were waiting their turn to board the ferry. Not even Elbridge Lowe said one word. They didn't want to gossip in Kate's presence. After reaching the other side, she noticed two wagons ahead of them were turning onto River Road. In addition, there were another two wagons coming from Sheet Harbour, waiting to turn down River Road as well. This was very unusual traffic.

"Oh, no!" Wayne exclaimed. "There's a traffic jam going up Cook Road. "Let us pass," he yelled. "Get out of the way, you're in the middle of the road." Wayne was trying his best to get to the Cooks' home.

Alexander knew why so many people were around but remained silent. He didn't want Kate to be hurt anymore.

Finally, they were inside, and then the eerie silence followed them inside the house. Her mother, Flo, was rocking back and forth in her rocking chair by the cook stove. She was turning her clasped hands over and over. Her hands were actually turning red. "Papa!" Kate ran to her father and they embraced each other. "What's going on?"

"I'm glad you're here, Kate. Come in," he gestured to Alexander, who was still standing by the door. "Sit down here at the table."

Kate noticed her father's voice had changed. He sounded so lost and lonely.

"Is it like this all the time?" Alexander gestured to the outside of the house while asking the question to Ed.

"I'm afraid so. It begins at dawn and goes until dark. Rain doesn't even stop them."

"What is it, Alexander?" Kate really didn't know.

"They want to see where the body was," Flo spoke but looked straight ahead. Kate approached the window to part the curtain to look outside. "No, Kate, close the curtain. I cannot stand to see them."

"It's okay, Mother. Alexander and I have come to take you to Watt Section."

"And not too soon." Alexander looked to Ed.

"I don't want to leave," Ed replied. "This is my home."

"You need to leave for Flo. She needs to be taken away from here."

*****

March 20, 1914, the day Sheet Harbour was abuzz with activity. Everyone in Sheet Harbour had been making plans for the last week or longer. Everyone had the same plan: get to Halifax for March 23rd.

All of Sheet Harbour was going to the murder trial. It seemed like everyone was going. The whole community was in celebration mode. The celebration began the night before, when a dozen or more coaster boats came into the harbour.

The *Chebucto* was the first to dock that morning at the wharf in West River. What a sight to behold -- three decks, lower, main, and upper. Her captain had sold every passenger space and a few more before noon. Mrs. Conrod was the first to meet her captain, for he booked a room at the Conrod House Hotel. He definitely was from the upper class. The only reason he was in a small town like Sheet Harbour was to make money.

The call had gone out that a good number of coaster boats were needed in Sheet Harbour. The *S.S. Dufferin*, smaller than the *Chebucto*, was also docked at the West River Wharf. *The Marlis* gave up her mail route to take passengers to Halifax and back. The *Sarah Lee.* The *Foaming Billow.* Any boat that could hold more than a dozen people was getting in on the celebration.

The captains were celebrating as well, for they were about to have lots of money in their pockets. They sold hundreds of passage tickets.

Every dock in Sheet Harbour was full of people lining up to get on a boat. The men wore their best pants and shirts.

The ladies had new dresses made for the occasion. The children that ran about in their Sunday clothes were told they would get a beating if they messed them up.

The people were prepared for anything. They had food and necessary items for three or four days. For no one knew how long the trial would be. It looked like a migration. Birds all going one direction. Every boat was full, some of them too full. Their destination was Halifax.

*****

Kate was not sitting on her rock by the lighthouse. She placed herself as far away as she could from Sheet Harbour Passage. Oh, yes, she heard the first boat pass by the lighthouse coming from Sheet Harbour. She could not help but hear. There was singing, fiddle music, and dancing; it could be heard for miles over the water. Alexander told her it was the *Chebacto*, one of nicest coaster boats in Nova Scotia. If the *Chebacto* was here for any other reason, Kate may have taken more notice, but the *Chebacto* was leading the way to a murder trial, her brother's murder trial. She went to her bedroom. She closed the windows and the flowered curtains. She climbed into her bed, pulled the matching flowered quilt up as far as it would go, and then, to drown out any sound, she added the pillow over her head.

The children, oh to be a child again. They were at the lighthouse taking it all in. They didn't know what all of this meant. The rest of the family was in the parlour. Elizabeth was sitting in her chair with her knitting. Ed and Flo were both on the settee; Flo also forced herself to knit. Alexander was sitting in the captain'' chair. As usual, he didn't feel like a captain. He had nothing to say. Actually, no one was talking. All that could be heard was the clicking of the knitting needles, and, of course, the singing, and music. They were not children, and they knew what all this meant. This was the day before the dreaded trial.

Chapter Fifteen

A Ballad Written in Blood

Cold, sticky darkness covered Edward. His breathing laboured, Edward sat staring out the small window searching for any glimmer of light. Not one star could be seen. As a young boy, he could stare at the sky and count the stars until dawn. Not tonight. The only light was from a streetlight on the wharf, a spider web of light glowing in the distance. But even it was being engulfed by the clouds. The fog appeared more like white clouds to Edward, low and covering the city like a shroud. The night was cold and wet, but it was not the weather that sent more than one shiver down his back, causing him to shift a little in his chair. "It's all over now; the end is near." He spoke aloud, but there was no one to hear him. He started to sing, "Rock of Ages, cleft for me, let me hide myself in Thee." When he finished the familiar hymn, he sat straighter in his chair, reached out his hand, and pulled a short chain on the small lamp sitting on the table.

As his gaze returned to the window, he saw a man looking back at him. Edward stared at the man for some time. He could swear the man was laughing. He shook his head, focusing once again on the man. They were staring at each other. Edward hardly recognized himself. *Was it just the other day?* Patrick brought a barber through those doors. He seemed to be a nervous little man, but before leaving, he had fixed Edward up really nice. Short hair, no beard. Patrick also bought him new pants, new shirt. He even bought new underwear. They had sat folded neatly untouched on the table for two days. Edward had been instructed they were to be worn only on the day of the trial. Patrick was making sure Edward got the message.

Edward got the message. That was several days ago. None of it had mattered. Not the short hair, not the shave, not the new clothes. He knew he wouldn't like the judge the moment he entered the courtroom. The judge didn't even look at Edward. Edward didn't like it, but what he didn't know was the judge never looked at the accused. He had learned early on to keep a distance. It helped the judge sleep at night. The judge just floated his way up the stairs to his bench. His black robe sailed along with him. As the judge sat down, Edward stifled a laugh. He didn't know if anyone else had noticed the judge's hand go to his head, trying to keep his white wig from falling off. He tried to have more control, for he knew everyone in the crowded gallery was watching every move he made.

The prosecutors were well prepared. Even Edward thought they had done a bang up job. If they had not been talking about him, he would have been cheering them on. They began with a member of the family of the slain man -- Sadie Asaff, the peddler's sister. Edward had thought immediately of Kate, searching the courtroom for his own sister. Relief swept over him as he discovered she was not there. *Good. I'm glad she stayed home.*

The prosecutor took a wallet from a box on his table. He handed it to Sadie. "Have you seen this wallet before?"

"Yes, sir, that wallet belongs to my brother, or it did belong to my brother. But he's gone now, isn't he?" Tears were collecting at the edges of Sadie's dark eyes.

"Yes, Sadie. May I call you Sadie?"

Sadie answered by nodding her head. She was trying to regain her composure.

"Do you need some time, Sadie?" The prosecutor wanted his witness to be alert.

Sadie again answered by moving her head. This time she shook it back and forth and replied, "No, sir, I have been waiting a long time to speak about my brother Charles. That's the least I can do for him now."

"Tell me about the wallet, Sadie."

"Like I said, this is my brother Charles' wallet. I've seen it many times. Of course, he carried his money in it."

"Thank you, Sadie, you can step down now. Be careful of the two steps; don't fall."

Edward was thinking aloud. "I should have left that wallet behind. But it was a very nice wallet, leather; it was made of leather. . ."

"What did you say, Edward?" O'Hearn leaned his way.

Edward remained silent. He remained silent, while all those who knew him testified against him. Edward couldn't believe how many from Sheet Harbour got up on that stand. He lost count after twenty-five. He knew them all, and they stared right through him. Edward thought it was never going to be over. Then the prosecution ended with the peddler's brother, Joseph Asaff.

Now it was his council's turn to call their witnesses. They didn't have even one witness to call.

Judge Ritchie began instructing the jury. Edward didn't hear much of what he said. He had already tuned out everything way before the judge began to speak. Nevertheless, he came to attention when he heard him talking about the cheque.

"(T)hree different stories[vii] – got it from the peddler, the old man, his uncle, got it from Murphy for working for him, then he got it from Murphy himself. Of course, he lied about it. . . "

Of course, I lied about it. Murphy never did work for me. I was not very smart telling three stories.

"But you don't punish him for that." Judge Ritchie continued to address the jury. "You don't find him guilty because he is a liar, but you say to yourselves from the conduct of this man. . ."

That's right; you can't find me guilty just because I am a liar. Edward was paying more attention to what this judge was saying.

"(F)rom the different stories hc has told as to the possession of the post office order, are we irresistibly drawn to the conclusion that he murdered this man? That is for you to decide. Of course, if he had given any reasonable explanation for it, that would have disposed of it. If he had stuck to his story that he got it in change, and if he had called his aunt and his uncle to produce the goods that he bought from the peddler, there would have been an explanation. It is for you to say what inference you draw from it."

I couldn't stick to my story. My story came to a brick wall. Edward's mind left the courtroom again.

The jury had already retired to deliberate. After a moment of conversation, Ritchie came down with his gavel so hard that Edward wondered what O'Hearn had said. Bang! The gavel sounded again. Ritchie spoke with a loud voice, "Declined!"

After O'Hearn sat down in his chair, Terrill leaned over asking a question, "What was that all about?"

"All I was trying to get across to him was he forgot to tell the jury the whole trial was based on circumstantial evidence. I asked for the jury to be brought back in to hear this. You heard what happened."

It wasn't long before the jury came back in. In fact, not many had even exited the courtroom. Everyone sat back down in their seats.

"John W. O'Neil, do you speak for the jury?" the judge asked the man.

"Yes, sir, I do."

"Has the jury reached a verdict?"

"Yes, sir."

"And what is that verdict?"

John W. O'Neil looked down at his paper. "Guilty, with a very strong recommendation to mercy."

A cheer went up throughout the whole gallery, like the audience's reaction to a prizewinner fight at a sporting event. It was a knockout; everyone was on their feet cheering.

"Order in the Court!" was repeated several times, as Edward's council and police quickly escorted Edward out of the courtroom, back to his jail cell, if you could call it a jail cell.

Edward was looking out of the dark wet window, seeing his reflection, a reflection of a guilty man. Were those tears or just the rain falling on the windowpane?

Edward shook his head to clear his mind. He reached for his pencil, opened his writing tablet, and looked over his notes. He read the last line he had written; it must have been weeks ago.

. . . The heavy swing of a sharp keen axe

He put his pencil into his mouth. Looking at his reflection one more time, he turned to his writing tablet and began to write.

He died an unknown death.

When he shall say depart from me,

With Satan for to dwell

Oh you who did this wicked crime

In burning flames of hell.

With sorrowful heart and blood stained hand

And on that gallace high

To pay that heavy penatte

I am condemned to die.

Now all kind hearted men and boys

As you roam from place to place

Never do as I have done

Your people to disgrace.

I lived a bad and reckless life

Till I became a man

If I had died in my mother's arms

I'd never have killed that man.

I pray to God both night and day

As I am bound in iron cell

To bring the one I layed to life

And take my soul from Hell.

I never shall regain my soul

Which I've helped to stain,

Both for spilling the blood

of an innocent man

I am guilty alas and doomed.

I hold the hand of a fair young girl

Brought up in Elms Park

Till I became a murderer

Which caused us both to part.

She wept and cried most bitter

Tears from her eyes did flow

To think that I committed murder

And to the gallace go.

May God protect my only girl

To her I brought the shame

So Good by friends around me

I'll bid my last farewell.

I never met you in this world

Nor in the world to come

I'll die a guilty murderer

Bound to speechless shame.

Edward jumped. The sound of a key turning in the door across the room startled him. Who was coming? Again, he quickly closed his notepad and placed the pencil on top.

"Edward, I came to visit." Reverend Rogers swept into the room ahead of Patrick.

"Just bang on the door when you are ready to leave." Patrick was already closing the door and locking it.

"That will be fine, Patrick." Rogers was halfway across the room towards Edward.

"I didn't think I would see you today." Edward wasn't sure he was in the mood for a visit to cheer him up.

"I heard the trial didn't end well for you. I thought you might want someone to talk to."

"You and I have talked about how the trial would go. Nothing surprised me."

"God still loves you. You have come a long way, Edward. These last few months you have learned that God indeed loves you."

"That's the only thing I do know right now: God loves me. Thank you for showing me this. You have become a good friend to me."

"Is there anything I can do for you?"

"You've done everything that needs to be done."

Chapter Sixteen

A Wallet or a Purse?

O'Hearn ran his hands through his hair. He stared at the picture on the wall in his office. It was a picture taken by the famous photographer, MacAskill, of the *Bluenose*, Nova Scotia's pride and joy. The greatest schooner ever built. The *Bluenose* was the fishermen's best friend. She was used by them just off the coastline of Nova Scotia to catch fish. After the fishing was done, the race was on for all the schooners, for the first one back to shore would get the highest price for their fish. This is where the *Bluenose* became famous. She always won; she would be home hours before any other schooner. She always got the top dollar for fish. She was fast, and nobody could keep up with her, for she sailed like the wind.

"Now, what are we going to do?" James Terrell knew he was only the assistant to Edward's lawyer, O'Hearn. Terrell waited to see if O'Hearn had any tricks up his sleeve.

"I have no idea." O'Hearn tore his gaze from the *Bluenose* picture. He didn't have any winning plan to offer.

"Don't give up yet! I'm not becoming a criminal lawyer for nothing," Terrell declared. He had not worked so hard to get on this case for nothing.

"They certainly tore Edward Cook apart yesterday. There is not much to work on." O'Hearn remained worried.

"You're correct. Therefore, we don't go that direction. We go for the mistrial."

"The what?" O'Hearn moved his chair closer to his desk. He placed his elbows close to the centre, very close to Terrell, who sat facing him.

"Mistrial, which is all we have to go on. Didn't you see me taking notes during the trial?"

"Yes, and I thought you were writing a letter to your grandmother."

"Thanks for your high opinion of me."

O'Hearn threw his arms up in the air. "We didn't have much else to do."

"I wasn't writing to my grandmother, may her soul rest in peace. I believe we have a good case, well, maybe not a good case, but a fair case for a mistrial."

"Now, I have to hear this. Continue. Don't let me interrupt."

"To begin with, Ritchie wouldn't even allow us to quote another case. The reason he said was it had nothing to do with this case. You saw what happened when the jury left the room; you approached the judge. He addressed the jury, but didn't say that the whole trial was drawn on circumstantial evidence. You requested the judge to recall the jury and further charge them that they must not only find the evidence consistent with the prisoner's guilt, but they must also be satisfied that the evidence was inconsistent with any other explanation, theory, or hypothesis. The judge wouldn't even think about it. He made it clear he wouldn't think about it when he came down with his gavel hard to make the point. Then he declined."

"I believe Ritchie misdirected the jury by failing to leave to them the issue whether the deceased, Asaff, was killed deliberately or accidentally."

"Yes, but. . ." O'Hearn interrupted for the first time. "Richie did remind the jury that the prisoner must be acquitted, if they were not convinced beyond a reasonable doubt."

"However, he left out the deliberately or accidentally." Terrell looked down at his notes. "Oh, yes, here is a good one. I wrote it down as soon as I heard it. The judge called the wallet a purse, several times."

"That sure is a technical point." O'Hearn was beginning to have doubts.

"I have seen trials thrown out for less technical points than that. We have to try something. We can't let this Cook be the first man hanged under the new laws."

"You mean no public hangings?"

"Yes, and you saw how the people in the gallery acted when the verdict came down. They wanted something to party about."

O'Hearn turned to Terrell. "You write it up, and we will deliver it in the morning. We may be grasping at straws, but better than no straws."

*****

O'Hearn was actually running down the sidewalk towards his office building. He took the concrete steps two at a time, leading to the double front doors. Everyone looked his way as he flew by.

"Where is Terrell?"

The secretary pointed towards Terrell's office. "In there, sir."

"Good." O'Hearn didn't have a minute to lose. He opened the door and shut it with a bang. "Terrell, we may have something." Finally, O'Hearn fell into a chair facing him.

"Really, what has happened? Terrell had never seen O'Hearn so animated, for everyone knew O'Hearn was a quiet man.

"You know the date of the sentencing?"

"Courthouse tomorrow afternoon at 2 p.m."

"It has been cancelled." O'Hearn gasped for air. He didn't realize how out of breath he was.

"Cancelled?"

"Yes, the judge is sick. So he has put it off for several days."

"And you ran in here to tell me that? Is this good or bad, for us I mean?"

"Good, good, good. Very good."

"How is that?" Terrell was not putting the pieces of the puzzle together very well.

"He cannot do that. He cannot change the date of sentencing, at least without an application to the Privy Council[viii] for special leave. He hasn't done that."

"You finish the application for a Crown Case Reserved[ix]. I see you are working on it now. I will make an application to the Court en banc.[x]"

Terrell put his ink pen in the inkwell. "While you are here, I have also been doing some study on cases. We can make an appeal to discharge the prisoner, made on the grounds that the evidence was not sufficient to support a conviction. I will also prepare that to be given to Ritchie."

*****

A week later, O'Hearn, Terrell, and Judge Ritchie were sitting in a wainscoted, polished, mahogany room. It looked more like a great sailing ship, rather than a judge's chambers. The leather chairs squeaked, as the two men slid into them. Both O'Hearn and Terrell were facing Judge Ritchie.

Terrell couldn't help noticing that Ritchie looked a lot thinner without his black robe. Plus, his hair, there was hardly any, only what circled a very shiny bald spot. No wonder he didn't want his white wig to fall off at court.

"Gentlemen, thank you for coming. I know your time is of great value, but mine is even greater. So, let us get right to the point. Shall we?"

Terrell and O'Hearn nodded their heads in agreement. Ritchie didn't wait for a reply.

"I have read and studied your two applications." Ritchie had them in front of him. "I have taken it upon myself to ask two colleagues, sound judges of our court system to help me with the information and how to address this, if I address it at all. Your motion to discard the prisoner, made on the grounds that the evidence was not sufficient to support a conviction. Several judges went through the case. The judges unanimously turned down the motion.

"As for the Application to the Court en banc, I believe the subject was my illness. Nasty cold that was. I think an application to the Privy Council for special leave would be a frivolous application, and, therefore, I will not grant a reprieve. This is a point, purely technical in character, and one in which the guilt or innocence of the prisoner is not involved.

"I do have discretion to grant a reprieve under section 1063. I would hesitate a long time before I exercised that discretion in favor of this prisoner who has been properly convicted of murder in cold blood in order to steal.

"Application denied and dismissed. Gentlemen, good day." At this dismissal, Ritchie left the room, closing the door behind him, leaving O'Hearn and Terrill staring at one another.

*****

The courtroom was empty. That is, except for Edward and his council, and the prosecution, which had several lawyers on the other side of the room. The last time they were in this room, it was crowded. That was then. This is now. This gathering is for the sentencing. What would they do to Edward Cook?

Judge Ritchie, back in his black robe and white wig, was sitting at his bench, above everyone else. He stood to address those standing before him. He didn't look at Edward.

"The sentence of the court is that the prisoner be taken to the prison whence he came and there confined according to law, and that on the 30th day of June next he be hanged by the neck until he be dead; and may God have mercy upon his soul."

*****

It was final. Edward knew the end had come. For the third time, he picked up his pencil and opened his writing tablet. He wanted to make sure he finished this. Maybe it would actually help someone. He read his poem from the beginning to the end. At least to where he had stopped the last time. Again, his hand began to write:

> *The sentence is passed upon me*
>
> *The time is drawing nigh*
>
> *The gallace high remains for me*
>
> *The thirteenth day of June.*
>
> *High on the scaffold there I'll stand*
>
> *For the deed which I have done*
>
> *Surrounded by a canvas wall*
>
> *Till the fatal trap is sprung.*

The rope is placed upon my neck

I shall breathe my last long breath

So good by friends and farewell all

I close my eyes in death[xi]

Edward began to look over what he had just written. Tears were falling on his paper. He picked up his pencil, and through the tears, he signed his name: Edward Cook. He closed his writing tablet, pushed his chair back, and stood. He crossed the room and lay down on the cot, his prison bed. Crossing his arms behind his head, he stared at the ceiling. Sleep would not come. He began to sing,

"Rock of Ages, cleft for me,
Let me hide myself in Thee."

It was very quiet in the office. So quiet the ticking of the clock on the wall sounded like drums beating. Instead of tick tock, it sounded like bang, bang over and over again. Terrell was sitting at the desk with many books opened around him. "There has got to be something we have missed. Something we can do." Terrell was not giving up yet. He didn't like to lose. "Here it is, the last thing we can do. An application made to the Governor-General-in-Council[xii] for executive clemency[xiii]. I will have it sent to Ottawa first thing in the morning."

A reply never arrived in time.

*****

Patrick put the key into the door for the last time. His hand was not shaking, nor did he have any anxiety about opening the door. He tried his best not to, but after each time he spoke to Edward, he grew to like the man. Edward didn't act like a murderer, not that Patrick knew any other murderer. However, Edward was kind, even the preacher, the Reverend Rogers, who visited daily, said he was kind. Edward was always singing hymns. How can a murderer praise God?

I guess he has changed, Patrick was thinking to himself. *Now they are going to hang him.* He felt really bad. However, Edward had told him not to feel bad. Edward had expressed his hope that someone would learn from him. He had even added that he prayed men would follow Jesus instead of the devil.

Reverend Rogers was praying with Edward when the door opened. Patrick waited until he heard, "Amen." Then he approached Edward. "Is there anything you want me to do for you this evening? Before tomorrow, you know."

"Thank you, Patrick, you have become a good friend. I never had very many friends, and I count you one. Reverend Rogers has agreed to stay with me."

*****

June 30, 1914.

The next morning just before the appointed time, Edward handed his writing tablet to his friend Reverend Rogers.

Then he was led away.

Chapter Seventeen

A New Family Bible

Kate was in bed and had been there since the verdict of the trial came down. The pain was so great she didn't know if she could handle it. The world had stopped; she didn't know anything that was happening around her. Everything was a blur. Someone had fed the children and had taken care of the daily chores. She never asked who did it.

One day, she was awakened very early. The sun was shining through a tiny space in the curtain from the window. The birds could be heard singing, even though the window was shut tight. It was July. She opened the curtains wide and stood there a very long time, taking in the view around her. No one could capture the moment she was experiencing. No artist was good enough. It was just too beautiful. She looked beyond the lighthouse at the sparkling blue ocean. Her eyes focused closer towards the shore, where she could see seagulls following the fishermen in their boats. They were heading out to search for their daily catch. The seagulls were calling after them to have a safe journey and return soon. The field in front of the lighthouse was white with a sea of daisies swaying in the gentle ocean breeze. Daisies were Kate's favourite flower. She would take the children and lay a blanket in the field of white. They would lie on their backs, looking up at the clouds as they journeyed out over the ocean. She smiled as she recalled making daisy chains, placing them in the girls' hair. The barn swallows were flying here and there, catching any flying insects that happened to be there.

That is when it hit Kate. Everything was beautiful, and she could feel herself being happy again. Kate knew what she was going to do. This was the answer to the question that repeatedly was inside her head. She was going to be happy again. How could she be happy, knowing Edward had such a terrible ending to his life? She would go back to before all of the awful things had happened. Now she knew just how she was going to do it. No one could stop her. For sure not Maude. She didn't care about Maude. It was as if Maude never was. Kate didn't miss her one little bit. This was all Maude's fault. Someone had to be blamed and Maude fit the bill. She didn't like Edward, never did, well Kate didn't like Maude.

*****

Alexander was helping his mother prepare breakfast in the kitchen. She was far too feeble to do it alone. Elizabeth had stepped up when Kate took to her bed. Lloyd and Hazel were sitting at the table eating porridge. Erna was still too young to go to school, but she was sitting eating porridge too.

"Quickly, children, finish up. Wayne will be here shortly to take you to school."

"Grandmother," Lloyd looked up to Elizabeth, "how is Mother? The other two children were also waiting for the answer.

"She will be better soon. Don't worry, she will be fine. Now take your lunch pail and hurry." Elizabeth looked out the back door window. "Hurry, Wayne is at the well now." She could see Wayne had a small wagon with the new pony ready to go.

Lloyd and Hazel put their coats on, for it was still cool in the mornings. "Goodbye, Papa."

"Bye and be good," he answered.

The kitchen was very quiet, except for Erna drinking the last of her milk. Alexander put more strawberry preserves on his toast. "How long do you think it will take?" he looked towards his mother.

"Like I said, she will be better soon."

The very next moment they both looked up to the ceiling. "Sooner than you think," Elizabeth smiled, for they both heard someone stirring upstairs.

It was Kate, for she had opened her bedroom door and was walking on the landing before the stairs. She was surprised how weak she felt. She held tightly to the rail, as she slowly came down the stairs.

Kate stood in the doorway to the kitchen. Alexander pushed his chair out from the table and was on his feet. "Kate."

Elizabeth remained in her seat but smiled at Kate. "Do you want breakfast?"

"Sit here, Kate, beside me." Alexander had missed his wife being at the table for meals.

"I have decided what I'm going to do." Kate didn't mince words.

Both Alexander and Elizabeth were surprised, but they could see Kate seemed to be on a mission. She had the attention of both of them.

"I'm going to have a new life," Kate paused, looking for words to explain herself.

"What does that mean?" Alexander had concern written on his face. He pulled his chair closer to Kate and the table.

"Oh, don't worry; I'm not going anywhere. I'm going to rearrange my past life just a little."

"How?" Alexander still had that concerned look. Elizabeth just remained silent.

"Alexander, I want you to order me a new Family Bible. You know, one of those big ones. The kind you set on a table and everyone can see it."

"Why, don't we already have one?" Alexander was about to get up and bring it to her.

"Yes, we do," Elizabeth commented, remembering well how Kate had helped her fill out the new Bible after the great fire.

"Sit down, Alexander. I don't need to see that Bible. I know what I'm going to do. I'm going to take people out of our Family Bible. From this day forward, Edward's name will not be there. In addition, Maude's name will be erased. From this day forward, the name Edward and the words murder, trial, hanging, will never be spoken in this house or in this family."

"Do you agree? If not, I will surely die."

"Agreed." Elizabeth found her voice. "Except for one thing: you cannot erase Maude's name, for she is your sister."

"I never want to see my sister again. As far as I'm concerned, I have no sister."

"You may change your mind, Kate." Alexander didn't know what to think about what his wife was proposing.

Kate looked straight at Alexander. "And from this day onward, you and everyone else will call me Catherine. Kate has died. From this day forward, I will have a new life. I will bury my history so deep no one will ever find it. I only look to the future."

What could they possibly say? Kate looked like she meant every word she said.

"Kate." Elizabeth wanted to change the subject. "Kate, we need to get you better. Staying in bed as long as you have has left you weak, and your face looks white and peaked. We can talk about all your plans later. Let us start now with a good breakfast. Catherine, she had already agreed to the change of name. Catherine, there is porridge here." She gestured to the cook stove. "Would you like a bowl?"

"Yes, I would. Thank you, Mother."

Catherine meant every word she had said. When the new Bible arrived, she started in earnest to change parts of her history. Elizabeth took the time to help. After the children were in bed, they both sat at the dining room table. Elizabeth would read and Catherine would write in a beautiful handwriting. Edward Cook, born April 18, 1858, married to Flora Tilson McQuarrie, born July 11, 1860. Children. . . Elizabeth stopped. "Catherine, you cannot leave out Maude."

Catherine, with misty eyes, agreed. It was hard enough to erase Edward from her life. Maude would remain. Children: Eliza Alice Maude Cook and Catherine Deborah Cook.

Elizabeth looked up again. "If you're going to make changes to our history, so will I."

Catherine looked towards her husband's mother. "What would you ever change?"

"Heman's birth. I want to change Heman's place of birth to Cork, Ireland. He had close ancestors there."

It was done. They made their family history the way they wanted it. From that day forward, Edward was never mentioned again. From that day forward, Catherine didn't want a sister named Maude.

*****

Spring turned to summer and summer to fall. The orange maples tried to outdo the yellow maples. They never had a chance, because the red maples were so red that is all the people talked about. Even Wayne was heard to say, "Just look at that large maple tree. Have you ever seen anything so red?"

The children collected the coloured leaves. The red and, of course, the orange, and yellow. They had baskets full. They brought them to the kitchen, where Elizabeth showed them how to press them beneath two pieces of wax paper and then run a hot iron over them.

"Place them on the windowpane of your window, and throughout the winter, when the sun shines, the red, orange, or yellow will shine through."

Alexander joined the fun when he brought several pumpkins from the garden and placed them on the kitchen table. He showed Lloyd and Hazel how to make a Jack-O-Lantern.

Alexander looked towards his mother. "Shall I tell them the scary story about Jack?"

"I don't know. It may be too scary for Lloyd and Hazel, and for sure, little Erna."

Alexander turned towards his children. "Well, what do you think? Are you too little to hear a scary story?"

"No, Papa, no, Papa, we are not babies anymore." Lloyd was speaking for all."

"The story begins like this:

"This story is about a man named Jack. Jack was the meanest man in all of Ireland. He lived in a village not far from where I lived as a boy. If anyone ever dared to set foot on his land, he would catch them and put them in prison, where they would never see their families again. His neighbours knew he was a miserly, bad-tempered man, and stayed clear of him."

"Jack died and he stood outside the pearly gates. Saint Peter took one look at him and said, 'You cannot come into heaven. Mean, bad tempered men are not welcome here.' Then Jack stood by the gates of hell. Satan looked out at him. 'You are not welcome here. No one has ever tricked the devil, not until you. You have tricked me several times, and you are not good enough for hell. You are not welcome here.' "

"'What will I do?' Jack asked. 'If I'm not welcome in Heaven, and I am not welcomed in hell. What will I do?' "

"Satan answered, 'You will walk the earth forever with only a coal from hell to light your lantern.' However, Jack didn't have a lantern. All he could see were the pumpkins ready to pick in the cold field. He took a pumpkin and hollowed its centre out. He cut eyes, nose and a mouth, and then placed his coal from hell inside. The face shone through the pumpkin. A scary face it was. Jack, to this day, walks the earth, carrying his Jack-O-Lantern. On every October 31, children, to this very day, carve Jack-O-Lanterns to remind them never to be a miserly, bad tempered man or woman."

Alexander banged his hand down on the table. All the children squealed. Catherine's knuckles came up to cover a scream. "Alexander, you shouldn't scare the children so."

The story even scared Catherine, for she had never heard it. However, Wayne just smiled. He remembered well the day that Captain Heman told a room full of children in the playroom of that wonderful Show House. Then the fire, which destroyed that beautiful house. Wayne couldn't help thinking that life had its ups and downs. He was happy to still to be with the Kenney family, for it was a family he felt a part of. However, he could sense trouble ahead, for the Kenney family was starting a secret that would go beyond him and beyond Catherine. She believed that, if you didn't speak of something long enough, then that something never happened. Wayne felt a shiver go down his back as if a ghost just passed in front of him.

*****

"I have not seen Kate in months." Maude was speaking to John, as she poured strong black coffee into his mug.

"She wouldn't see you the last time you tried to drop by."

"Yes, she had taken to her bed and wouldn't see anyone. I was speaking to Papa when he dropped into the store last week."

John interrupted. "How is your mother?"

"Not well. She just sits in her chair, rocking back and forth. You and I know that nothing can be the same. Thanks to Edward, he has split the family into pieces. However, Papa said Kate seem to be doing better. He said something new was going on, for Kate insists on being called 'Catherine,' even Papa calls her Catherine now."

"If you go to visit, I would not speak of Edward or anything about the trial. It's still a sore spot to her and to your whole family that might rub salt into open wounds. You saw the article in the paper just a few weeks ago."

"I don't think they read the papers anymore. Except for that, one article they don't report on the murder case anymore. But they ended with a terrible story."

*****

Maude was correct when she said Catherine did not read newspapers any longer. But Elizabeth did. Not only did she read newspapers, but also she had letters weekly from Moses that kept her up to date on the trial and the hanging. Before Elizabeth read it in the newspaper Moses had written to her. The whole city of Halifax wanted to see the hanging of the murderer of the Syrian peddler. However, the law would deny them, for this was the first hanging that was not made public. The public was outraged, and to prevent riots, the body, after the hanging, was taken to a local funeral home for viewing. For three or four days, the public lined up to see the dead man. Moses wondered how many people from Sheet Harbour were in those lines.

Unless Catherine asked, Elizabeth didn't share the news from Moses, or the terrible stories that were printed in the newspapers.

Catherine did ask about the last stay Edward's lawyers had requested. They sent it to Ottawa. However, the hanging took place before a reply had been received. For this reason, Catherine believed they had hanged an innocent man. She was sure the last request for a 'stay,' especially sent to Ottawa, Canada's capital, would have set Edward free.

Catherine was so angry with her sister, Maude, for she had believed the reply would not have made a difference. They would still have hanged Edward.

Maude didn't yet know it, but as far as Catherine was concerned, when Maude made that statement, it would be the last time she would ever see or speak to her sister. In fact, she would begin to tell people she was not related to Maude in any way.

Every time Maude would try to visit her sister, Catherine, she was always dismissed. Catherine would not see her or her children.

Chapter Eighteen

The Journey Has Ended

I pulled my smartphone out of its case, which was sitting on the front seat of our car/truck. The engineer pulled on the horn of the train, taking away all other sound in the world around me. Waiting until the sound of the horn passed with the train, I hit the button, which would connect me to Paul. He answered on the first ring.

"Where are you?" he asked after I said hello.

"Waiting on a train, and it's a long one."

Paul could hear the clickety-clack as the heavy train cars passed in front of me.

"I may be another ten minutes at least."

"I'll have lunch ready when you get here."

"I will see you in a little bit. Love you. Bye."

Living in DeQuincy, Louisiana, a train town, you would think one would get used to the trains. I guess one does, I have. It wouldn't be DeQuincy without trains.

Looking around me, I could see all the American flags flying on all the telephone poles on 4th Street, the main street here in DeQuincy. Yesterday was the 4th of July, Independence Day. American flags are still flying everywhere.

July and, for that matter, August are my less favourite months of the year living in Louisiana. I get cabin fever, for I do not leave the house, or I try not to leave the house very often. Right now, looking at the dash of our car/truck, the temperature reads 98°, and add the humidity; the temperature feels like 108°. Thank God for air conditioning.

However, staying home gives me the opportunity to write. After placing this book on a shelf for six months, I pulled it down and have now completed it.

It has been five years since Paul and I backed that popup trailer into our yard. Five years since we unpacked all of our belongings. It has taken four years to renovate the house to make it the way we want it. It has been fun and we have enjoyed every minute.

But then something happened. I can quote Kate word for word in chapter 12 page 235. "It's funny how one minute your life is fine, and then you will never forget the next minute." Nothing will be the same. That's what happened when Alexander rushed back into the kitchen with snow flying all over the kitchen floor. "Come quick, there is something going on at your parents' house."

So many people can identify with that. I remember when this happened and everything changed. Catherine Wilcoxson and Catherine (Kate) Kenney experienced the same feelings. Nothing will be the same. I didn't have a sleigh come back; I did not have Alexander exclaim, "There is something going on at your parents' house."

No, my moment came by way of a phone call. It came on Boxing Day. You know the phone calls that say, "Are you sitting down." Then the person says, "Your child has been arrested and is now in jail." Not my child. My child is fine, a perfect child. We are proud of our child.

Tears have flown for two years 68 days and counting. We mark time with before the phone call and after. Just like Elizabeth and Alexander spoke of before the great fire and after.

I can understand why Catherine, my grandmother, wanted to start over. She made it happen. It lasted for three generations. She lived in a part of history that she thought it could be done. Just buy a new Family Bible. How easy could that be?

For me, history will not allow me to start over. I have to face the fact that I will parent an incarcerated son. He will be in prison for 18 years, most of the rest of my life. Except it could be worse; my son could be dead. He is not dead, not like Edward. We talk on the phone; we cry together. We correspond, he encourages me, and I encourage him. Life continues on.

Shame? Yes. Hurt? Very much so. Tears? An ocean full will fall.

This book is now done and the story ends. All the information I found in my research has been put into this story.

I still don't really know how birthdates and places were changed in the Family Bible. My aunts maintained to the day they died that the Family Bible was correct in telling the history of our family.

My father, Elbridge Reginald Kenney, Alexander and Catherine's fourth-born, was born right after Erna. The events of Edward and the events of Catherine starting a new life happened before he was born. I believe my father didn't know he had an Uncle Edward. He did know about an Aunt Maude, but little was ever said about her. Catherine and

Alexander had six more children, none of which knew about Edward. These six children married and had many children of their own, none of which knew of Edward.

It made me sad to be the one who uncovered the truth. Government records do not lie. If it had been just one record with mistakes, then I would have been happy to say the government of Nova Scotia made that mistake. That was not the case. This story is based on 90% documentation found in the archives of Nova Scotia, Canada. The information is there for anyone to see. If this book has troubled you, then I suggest you make a trip to the archives and start by looking up Edward Cook.

The hardest day of my research was the day I found *The Ballad of the Murder of Charles Asaff, a Syrian Peddler*. I read slowly through the hand-written verses. When I got to the end, it was signed in strong handwriting -- Edward Cook. Chills went down my back, and I cried out to Paul, "Look what I have found." I didn't expect it to be signed by Edward himself.

I read the hand-written notes from Edward's trial. The list of the people from Sheet Harbour who witnessed against Edward was right in front of me. Spending all my summers as a child in Sheet Harbour, I recognized most of the last names. As a child, I didn't know why some people didn't welcome me into their homes. They would not allow their children to play with me. Those very people's names were on the list. Maybe not their names directly, but their parents' names were there. Something was handed down from parents to children. I know not what.

I do remember Frannie Kenney. That would have been Maude's daughter-in-law. She always said we were related. She would tell anyone who would listen. Not very many people listened. My grandmother, Catherine, told me she was crazy and to stay away. I loved my grandmother, Catherine. In doing my research and talking with the older cousins, I realized I spent more time with Grammy Kenney (Catherine) than any other cousin did. I will carry those fond memories and stories with me forever. However, it is still sad to know that all of the older cousins and all of the younger cousins didn't get to know their grandmother's sister. Not just her sister, but also her sister's children and other blood relatives.

The time I spent in Nova Scotia during the summer of 2012 was the best trip we ever had, even if we did spend 89 days in a popup camper. I will never forget that trip. I got to spend the summer with my mother, Doris May McConaghy Kenney. She died the following spring, just before her 90th birthday.

That trip allowed me to do research to find out who Edward Cook was, and I also found Maude. I wish I could have known more of her family. That was taken away from me, a part of my history that is blank.

But why did Catherine do it? Was it shame about what her brother did? On the other hand, was it hurt, or a broken heart to see your loved one, your brother, have to suffer as he did?

We all want our lives to turn out well. Nevertheless, we cannot control that. I believe Catherine did what she did because she was hurt, not just the shame. Catherine's heart was broken.

Life continues on. Grammy Kenney lived a full life, far into her 80s. She lived with a secret, but secrets never remain secrets.

Sheet Harbour will never be the same for me. Almost everyone I know is gone.

We all have our sad stories to tell. The saddest story was how two sisters lived a lifetime without each other. Having sisters of my own, I can tell you how much they missed.

If only Catherine and Maude could have put the hurt behind them. If only Catherine could have forgiven. For forgiveness is what everyone needs to learn to do. Life would be so much better if we learned to forgive.

I don't hear Maude calling to me anymore. I believe Catherine and she are at peace.

But do not forget Maude and the Tale of these two Sisters.

Epilogue

The following is what was posted in the newspapers at the time of Edward's trial and after.

Guilty of Murder

Halifax. N.S., March 26.—Edward Cook, a young man, was found guilty of the murder of Charles Asaff. a Syrian peddler, at Sheet Harbor, N.S., last December. The trial was concluded last night. Asaff was shot through the head and robbed, and his body hidden under a pile of brush. The dead man's purse and a postal order were found on the prisoner. Cook received the verdict without emotion and was remanded for sentence.

Charles Asaff Murder in Winnipeg Free Press Friday, March 27, 1914.

Cook Confessed Before Going to Scaffold Today

Halifax, N. S., June 30—Halifax had its first hanging in 48 years, shortly after daylight this morning, when Edward Cook, Jr., 24 years of age, was executed for the murder of Charles Asaff, Syrian peddler, on Dec. 9, last at Sheet Harbor.

The drop was sprung by Executioner Holmes, and a few minutes after, life was pronounced extinct. Without a tremor Cook ascended the fifteen steps leading to the platform in which was placed the trap. He did not make a murmur as the lever was pulled.

Asaff, the peddler, who was murdered, was reported missing last December. Cook was arrested, a pocketbook and a money order belonging to Asaff being found in his possession.

He was found guilty, but before being sentenced, he made a statement implicating another man in the murder, but it was not accepted. After the execution this morning a confession made by Cook, three days ago was given out, stating that he alone had committed the crime, that nobody else was implicated and expressing his regret for any injury he had caused others.

Below is the story that occurred in the above newspaper clipping.

Medicine Hat News Newspaper Archive: June 30, 1914 - Page 1

Halifax, June 30.—Halifax had its first hanging in 48 years shortly after daylight this Morning, -when Edward Cook', Jr., 24 years of age, was executed for the murder of Charles Asaff, Syrian peddler, on Dec. 9 last at Sheet Harbor. 'The drop was sprung by executioner Holmes, and a few minutes after life was pronounced extinct. Without a tremor, Cook ascended the 15 steps leading to the platform in which was placed the trap. He did not make a murmur as the lever was pulled. Only the executioner, Rev. R. A Rogers, the jailer and the deputy sheriff were present at the real hanging, the scaffold being underneath canvas and the other officials and press representatives just outside until after the trap was sprung. Cook, during the last few days, has felt his position keenly and has taken great interest in the Bible. He slept from eight o'clock until midnight, and on awakening asked for his spiritual adviser. After the latter's visit, he paced up and down the cell for a time, then lay down and fell into a slumber. Again, just as day was breaking, Cook asked to see Rev. Mr. Rogers. Up to within a few minutes of the time, he went to the scaffold he was praying and singing hymns, and he went to the scaffold in an unconcerned manner. Asaff, the peddler, who was murdered, was reported missing 9th December Cook was arrested, a pocket-book and a money order belonging to Asaff being found in his possession. He was found guilty, but before being sentenced, he made a statement implicating another man in the murder, but it was not accepted. After the execution this morning a confession made by Cook, three days ago was given out, stating that he alone committed the crime, that no one else was implicated and expressing regret for any injury he had caused others.

ABOUT THE AUTHOR

Catherine Kenney Wilcoxson has many stories to tell, and tell them she must. Like the sea in her novels, Nova Scotia, calls to her, begging her to return. And like the gracious host her family and friends know her to be, she welcomes us along with her, giving us a taste of her childhood home. Whether you live in Sheet Harbour, or have never smelled the unmistakable north-Atlantic salt air, jump into her book, take a ride with Wayne on his wagon, and let the sea call you into a tale from the past. Catherine lives with her husband Paul in DeQuincy, Louisiana.

End Notes

---

[i] https://en.wikipedia.org/wiki/Keep_On_the_Sunny_Side

[ii] An abscess in the tissue around a tonsil usually resulting from bacterial infection and often accompanied by pain and fever "Quinsy." *Merriam-Webster.com*. Merriam-Webster, n.d. Web. 10 Nov. 2016.

[iii] A musical instrument of the lute family used in southwest Asia and northern Africa Oud." *Merriam-Webster.com*. Merriam-Webster, n.d. Web. 10 Nov. 2016.

[iv] A scow, in the original sense, is a flat-bottomed boat with a blunt bow, often used to haul bulk freight; *cf.* barge. The etymology of the word is from the Dutch *schouwe*, meaning such a boat. https://en.wikipedia.org/wiki/Scow

[v] *Sheet Harbour: A Local History* by James E. Rutledge, William Macnab & Son, Halifax. N. S. 1954, p.91

[vi] *Sheet Harbour: A Local History*, p. 90.

[vii] *The Eastern Law Reporter.* Volume 14. P. 481.

[viii] A privy council is a body that advises the head of state of a nation, typically, but not always, in the context of a monarchic government. The word "privy" means "private" or "secret"; thus, a privy council was originally a committee of the monarch's closest advisors to give confidential advice on state affairs. https://en.wikipedia.org/wiki/Privy_council

[ix] The Supreme Court of Nova Scotia, composed of a quorum of four judges only, has jurisdiction to hear and decide a Crown case reserved stated by the judge of the County Court Judges' Criminal Court for the opinion of the Supreme Court. (It is a form of appeal to a higher court composed of more

than one judged) https://scc-csc.lexum.com/scc-csc/scc-csc/en/item/15189/index.do

[x] en banc (on bonk) French for "in the bench," it signifies a decision by the full court of all the appeals judges in jurisdictions where there is more than one three- or four-judge panel. The larger number sit in judgment when the court feels there is a particularly significant issue at stake or when requested by one or both parties to the case and agreed to by the court. http://dictionary.law.com/Default.aspx?selected=625

[xi] MG 100, Vol 126 #10 and MG 100 Vol 86 No 39 Public Archives of Halifax, Nova Scotia, Canada .

[xii] Governor–general–in–council plural governors–general–in–council or governor–generals–in–council: the governor-general in a member nation of the British Commonwealth acting with the advice and consent of the nation's Privy Council usually as a formal means of giving legal effect to cabinet decisions <in South Africa ... all provincial ordinances must be assented to by the governor-general-in-council — Alexander Brady> "Governor–general–in–council." Merriam-Webster.com. Merriam-Webster, n.d. Web. 5 Dec. 2016.

[xiii] The Royal Prerogative of Mercy originates in the ancient power vested in the British monarch who had the absolute right to exercise mercy on any subject. In Canada, similar powers of executive clemency have been given to the Governor General who, as the Queen's representative, may exercise the Royal Prerogative of Mercy. It is largely an unfettered discretionary power to apply exceptional remedies, under exceptional circumstances, to deserving cases. https://www.canada.ca/en/parole-board/services/clemency/what-is-the-exercise-of-clemency-royal-prerogative-of-mercy.html